MURDER, MY LOVE

A MIKE HAMMER NOVEL

MORE MIKE HAMMER
FROM TITAN BOOKS

Lady, Go Die!

Complex 90

King of the Weeds

Kill Me, Darling

Murder Never Knocks

The Will to Kill

Killing Town

The Goliath Bone

The Big Bang (February 2020)

Masquerade for Murder (March 2020)

Kiss Her Goodbye (February 2021)

MURDER MY LOVE

A MIKE HAMMER NOVEL

MICKEY SPILLANE

and

MAX ALLAN COLLINS

TITANBOOKS

Murder, My Love: A Mike Hammer Novel
Print edition ISBN: 9781785655548
E-book edition ISBN: 9781785655555

Published by Titan Books
A division of Titan Publishing Group Ltd
144 Southwark St, London SE1 0UP

First edition: March 2019

1 3 5 7 9 10 8 6 4 2

A CIP catalogue record for this title is available from the British Library.

Printed and bound in the United States.

What did you think of this book? We love to hear from our readers. Please email us at readerfeedback@titanemail.com or write to us at Reader Feedback at the above address.

To receive advance information, news, competitions, and exclusive Titan offers online, please sign up for the Titan newsletter on our website: www.titanbooks.com

FOR ANDREW SUMNER –

Mike's man in the UK

CO-AUTHOR'S NOTE

Being chosen by Mickey Spillane to complete the surprising number of unfinished manuscripts he left behind is, for me, practically the definition of bittersweet. And it is definitely my greatest honor.

When I discovered Mickey's work I was around twelve—by way of the Darren McGavin TV series—and just starting to read the great hardboiled mystery writers. Dashiell Hammett and Raymond Chandler were first, followed soon by James M. Cain. I was able to start buying Mickey's Mike Hammer novels when I was thirteen, though I usually had to lie and pass myself off as sixteen. Spillane was thought of as writing "dirty books" back then, though many other storytellers have gone through the door he opened in a more explicit if less explosive fashion.

What remains shocking, in Spillane's work from the '40s through the '90s, is the extreme, convincing and often visceral scenes of violence. Sam Peckinpah, the great and notorious director of *The Wild Bunch*, had white hair, and I wouldn't be surprised if Mickey turned it that way for him, maybe with *One Lonely Night*, in which Mike Hammer, wielding a tommy gun, dispatches one hundred or so Commie spies.

Hammer was a character who grew and changed, as his creator sporadically recorded the detective's cases. The iconic private eye began as brash, excitable, randy as hell and not just a little psychotic. As the character aged, he mellowed; but a mellowed Mike Hammer can still appreciate a beautiful woman licking her lips and can dispatch a villain with chilling coldness.

The unfinished work Mickey bequeathed me (and his wife Jane) shows the author's own mellowing and the changes in his life. He was, at various times in his long career, a follower of the conservative Jehovah's Witness faith. Criticism from some in his church hampered Mickey's ability to tell the kind of tales expected of him. Often, during these periods, Mickey would begin a novel and then put it aside, when he decided someone high in his church might object.

His 1989 Hammer novel, *The Killing Man*, got him in dutch with the church elders because he used the words "shit" and "fucking" (sparingly) in the text. There wouldn't be another Mike Hammer novel published (one minus those offensive words) until *Black Alley* in 1996 (I completed his sequel, *King of the Weeds*, for Titan in 2014).

Jane Spillane reminded Mickey, a few days before his passing, that "Max isn't a Jehovah's Witness," and that I would almost certainly complete these novels in grand Spillane style—sex, violence, occasional "f" words and all. Mickey had no problem with that. He understood that we would be collaborating, and my sins would be my own.

In expanding Mickey's partial manuscripts into finished books, I first turned to material that was usually a hundred pages or more, often with plot and character notes. A dozen books or so later, I am now dealing with shorter fragments, and this time I am working only from a synopsis. As usual, I have done my best to determine when Mickey wrote the material, so that I might set each novel in continuity, to give each entry its rightful place in the canon.

The nature of the plot synopsis suggests it may have been designed for one of the Stacy Keach-starring *Mike Hammer* TV episodes or telefilms, which wrapped up in 1989 (revived in 1997). I know that Mickey developed several ideas for TV producer Jay Bernstein, and in fact *The Killing Man* began that way, until the story idea inspired Mike Hammer's creator to write a novel instead ("It was too good to waste on television," he told me). Mickey also devised the ending of the otherwise terrible, Bernstein-produced, non-Keach Hammer telefilm, *Come Die with Me* (1994), a production Spillane disavowed.

Part of my reasoning regarding the origin of the synopsis is that Mickey includes scenes in which Mike Hammer is not present, inappropriate for the first-person approach of the books, while the TV episodes sometimes featured such scenes. I have, of course, kept the point of view consistently Hammer's own in these pages.

The probable origin of the story makes this novel something of a departure, more typical of the TV series in that Hammer has a client, which he rarely does in the largely vengeance-oriented books. But as the plot here is predominantly the work of Hammer's creator, I trust readers will enjoy what might be viewed as a partial change of pace.

All of this suggests the intended time frame of the tale was the late '80s to the very early '90s. The political subject matter reflects Mickey's own distrust and even contempt for certain real-life figures of that era. Mickey and I did not entirely share political beliefs, which bothered neither of us a whit. We were friends, and we were pros—such a thing was irrelevant.

Besides, Jehovah's Witnesses don't vote.

Max Allan Collins
October 2018

CHAPTER ONE

The gray sky hanging over the city didn't promise rain. You couldn't make out any clouds in that slate dome, and only the sodden feel of humidity said that ashen sky might ever let loose. Was that the rumble of thunder getting itself in the mood, or the dissonant song of a distant train yard? Maybe all that gray would just turn into night; it had been this way since mid-afternoon and, in late fall, darkness came sudden.

The new Vankemp Building at sixty stories held up its shimmering middle finger to that gray sky and the gloom it threatened, or maybe to the ghosts of those who'd dwelled in the tenements such new buildings displaced, the sweatshop workers and their progeny who had made the original Vankemp richer than sin. Such staggering wealth Thadeous Vankemp's great-great-grandchildren still shared, including the famous socialite Nicole Vankemp, even as the causes she championed may have made the old boy spin in his fancy marble mausoleum.

Fighting for women's rights, campaigning against land mines and throwing AIDS fund-raisers? How *could* she?

And beautiful Nicole's brand of sin was nothing old Thadeous would have recognized—free love, Park Avenue style, including one lover who she told *Vanity Fair* was "a Nijinsky of cunnilingus."

Nor would the original Vankemp likely appreciate this new glass-and-steel monolith on Fifth Avenue bearing the family name. He and others with the famous surname had seen very different buildings go up in the 1900s into the 1930s, buildings that still dominated Manhattan today—edifices with architectural dignity, reflecting the stature of the men they'd been named for. Not a giant glass tombstone.

No question about it. Once you die, you really start losing control of things.

The sky rumbled again and the vast gray ceiling bore darker patches now. I shrugged the collars of my trenchcoat up and tugged my porkpie fedora down. I looked like a refugee from some old private-eye paperback cover, which is what I was. You had to have an image to make it, and maintain it, in New York, New York, the city so nice they got redundant about it. The shamus schtick was mine, my coat and hat like the dirty talk and public service characterizing that Nicole dame.

I might be meeting her tonight. Cunnilingus wasn't on the menu, but you never knew what might get served up in this town. Of course, her husband was who I was meeting, in his office on the top floor of this not-open-to-the-public-yet building. Hell, right now it was just this shiny slab rising out of a work site, no landscaping yet, just rough, clod-flung earth decorated with everything a worker might need from a wheelbarrow to a crane, from a pile of sheetrock to a Caterpillar tractor.

I found my way to the gate in the chain-link fence. I was

expected, but I still had to yell at the security guy in a uniform as gray as the sky. I showed him the badge and the operator's ticket in the leather fold. He had the look of a cop who retired and then boredom set in, or maybe a pension just wasn't cutting it. Which had put him back on the job. Sort of.

"Michael Hammer," he said, reading. He had a face like an old catcher's mitt that had caught a couple eyeballs. "You wouldn't be *Mike* Hammer, would you?"

"Yeah. Mr. Winters is expecting me."

"He *said* a Mr. Hammer would be around."

"Well, I'm Mr. Hammer."

"I didn't know Mike Hammer was still alive!"

"Think of my surprise."

Grinning, he let me in, locked the gate behind us, and led me down a gravel path through the construction site to the building. He was chatty but wasn't asking questions, so I didn't have to listen.

He unlocked one of the half dozen glass doors fronting the place. He was smiling as he opened it for me, shaking his head. "Mike Hammer, still above ground. Who'd have thunk it? You used to be in the papers."

"So was Happy Hooligan."

"I remember that comic!"

I was almost inside when he blurted, "Hey! You still pals with Captain Chambers? He still on the job?"

"Yeah," I said, figuring it covered both questions.

"Tell him Murphy said hello. He'll remember!"

"Sure." After all, how many cops named Murphy could there be on the NYPD?

All the fresh building odors were waiting, as unmistakable as new car smell. Glue and paint and putty and grout, all mixed up in an olfactory cocktail. What would soon be a gleaming tiled lobby looked even larger minus any furnishings, dirtied up by occasional footprints and areas where finishing touches were yet to be made.

The bank of elevators, with shiny steel doors bearing occasional dirt smears and handprints, maintained the same almost complete but untidied status. I pushed the button, the door slid immediately open and I stepped on. To gain access to the sixtieth floor required a key. I'd been sent one. Jamie Winters himself had called me and I asked why we were meeting in a building not yet open to the public.

"It's a secure location," the smooth, familiar baritone stated, over the phone.

I asked, "Don't you have your office swept for bugs, regularly?"

"I do."

"So do I."

"I'm sure that's so, Mr. Hammer. But not for your *own* devices."

The senator was no dummy. I had the capacity to record client meetings, all right, and I almost always did. Velda, my secretary who is the other licensed P.I. of MICHAEL HAMMER INVESTIGATIONS, keeps the current tapes in the office wall safe and the rest in a safe deposit box.

I considered wearing a wire to this meet, just to have a record of it, and say a silent "screw you" to my celebrated client. But I skipped it. He wanted privacy and I'd go along.

I stepped off the elevator on the sixtieth floor. The unfinished nature of the building was even more obvious here, the floor lacking carpet, the ceiling unfinished with wiring hanging like the veins and arteries of a body opened up in an autopsy. Windows at either end of the hall were minus glass and instead covered in heavy plastic sheeting that pulsed with wind. The open space I'd entered appeared to be set aside for a reception area.

A mahogany door, center stage, had a nameplate that read SENATOR JAMIE B. WINTERS, a firm declaration in the midst of incomplete surroundings.

I knocked and said, "Mike Hammer, Senator!"

"Come in, Mike!"

That was a typical politician's phony familiarity—we'd never met and on the phone had addressed each other as "Mister."

I went in and the coldness of the night was waiting. The sidewalls would be windows onto the city, but right now were just rectangles of duct-taped plastic, trembling and crackling in the wind. The office, like the hallway, was unfinished, the ceiling tile uninstalled, more innards-like wiring lurking above, and a few bare temporary light bulbs hanging, more suited for a flophouse hallway. Like a parody of the fancy desk that would be installed before long, a chunk of plywood rode two sawhorses with Senator Winters seated behind it on a metal stool.

Two more such stools waited, facing him like clients' chairs. On the makeshift desk sat an ashtray with a cigarette burning, and next to that a bottle of Canadian Club and another of Canada Dry. Three glasses, in hotel-style wrappers, were on the plywood, too.

"I understand," the senator said, "Canadian Club and ginger is your drink."

"That or Miller Lite."

Jamie Winters got up and came around and extended a hand

as if pointing to where a tree should be planted. He was boyishly handsome and looked about thirty-five, though I knew him to be eight years past that. His dark brown hair was medium on top and short on the sides, a cut that would've cost him a C-note at least. His olive shoulder-padded blazer was unbuttoned over a black silk t-shirt, and his blousy, pleated chinos were a matching olive—an ensemble as casual as it was expensive.

His shake was firm, not sweaty at all, and he had the kind of white smile and perfect teeth that cost real money.

While he got back behind his plywood desk, I tore off the wrapper on a glass and poured myself a drink. "You don't need me," I told him.

"Why is that?"

I shook my head, got myself perched on the stool. "Sounds like you already have an investigator on staff, if you know what I drink."

His smile really was a dazzler, but I could already see the troubled man behind it—the eyes, as olive as the suit, gave it away.

His padded shoulders shrugged. "I just called my clipping service and they put something together on you. You were really something, back when."

"Yeah. In my impetuous youth, I racked up what they call these days a substantial body count."

He worked to make his reply sound off-hand. "Mobsters, mostly, right? But sometimes just plain killers."

I shook my head again. "No such thing. Killers come in all shapes, sizes and sexes."

"Is that so, Mr. Hammer?"

The voice decidedly female, though it was almost low enough to be male.

I hadn't heard her come in, but don't figure me for losing my edge—it was the flap of plastic non-windows and the wind whistling behind them that covered for her.

So I took a chance and showed off a little. With my back still to her, I said, "That's right, Mrs. Winters."

Then I turned to get a look at her, where she stood just inside the office.

I said to her, "I've killed men and I've killed women. One man was even dressed as a woman. There was a kid once, and a 'special needs' case, you'd call him. No 'just plain killers' in the bunch."

She moved like sex on springs, a tall, lithe woman in a black leather catsuit that zipped up in front and lacked only a whip for the S & M crowd to go all giggly. The size of those thrusting breasts was wrong for the otherwise fashion model frame, but what the hell—nobody's perfect.

But her face was. Perfect. Big green eyes, dark eyebrows that were full and real and arching, high cheekbones, and blazing red hair that was a damn mane of the stuff, tumbling to her shoulders, brushing her forehead, as if it just happened that way and wasn't the work of a hairdresser whose hourly rate was probably twice mine.

Oh, and her lips. A wide mouth, probably too wide, but my God so full and moist. Was that dark red, almost black lipstick in fashion? Not that I gave a damn.

They said Senator Winters was headed for the White House.

But we never had a First Lady who looked like this. Not even Jackie Kennedy. And Nicole Vankemp-Winters sure wasn't Mamie Eisenhower.

At the plywood-plank desk, she unwrapped a glass and poured herself a drink, twitching a smile at her husband. He looked at her almost greedily, like he knew what he had. Maybe he did.

Then she unwrapped another glass and built her hubby one. Everybody was having what I was.

"My husband," she said, in her Lauren Bacall purr, turning my way, "tells me the clippings say that you have more killings to your credit than—"

"I don't think 'credit' is the word."

She finished her thought: "More killings to your credit than any other living man."

"Civilian killings," I corrected.

"Explain, Mike. You don't mind the familiarity?"

"There's a distinction, Nicole... no, I don't. Plenty of combat soldiers, and I was one for a while, racked up more notches than I ever did, on their belts or their guns or whatever. Audie Murphy took out two-hundred-and-forty and that's strictly Germans. The Sicilians were just gravy."

I was really only fucking with her, but I saw something in her eyes that disturbed me. Like the smells in the unfinished lobby, it was a cocktail of things—fear, excitement, anticipation.

I finished the CC and ginger and stood. "Okay, I think we're done here."

They both looked alarmed, and exchanged glances to that effect, and then the senator was on his feet. He had a decent build under those loose olive threads and that black t-shirt. These two were prime specimens, all right.

Winters said, "We're just getting started, Mr. Hammer."

"No. What you want is a hit man. I don't kill people for money. It's more for... sport."

They both looked afraid now. Good.

But just between us, it's never been for sport. It's been to settle scores and balance the scales of justice, when the system screwed up, or I craved the satisfaction.

"I don't like murder," I said. "I put up with a lot out of people— humanity as a species is no prize... yet I have this old-fashioned respect for human life, anyway, that might seem..."

"Hypocritical?" she asked, arching a brow.

"Paradoxical," I said. "You can't imagine how many people I've killed. Most of 'em haven't made the papers. But the people I took out, well... all put together? Collectively, they'd have gone on to kill far more than I ever managed."

"You sound," she said dryly, "like a pest control man."

"Sometimes it works out that way," I said with a shrug. "But you people seem to expect me to kill somebody for you. Well, I don't do that anymore. Not so much, anyway."

She put a hand on my arm. The full breasts under the black leather seemed to move of their own accord. She had my attention.

"Sit down, Mike," she said. "We don't want a hit man. And what we're interested in is not the way you handle your enemies with... such ruthless dispatch. But rather..."

"...your reputation," her husband said, sitting down again, "for coming through for your clients."

The wind was playing banshee beyond the plastic windows.

Winters got out a pack of Salems, offered me one, and I raised a hand in a "pass" gesture.

"Everybody knows Mike Hammer smokes," he said with a smile.

The clipping service again.

"I gave it up," I said. "A couple of times, but it finally took. That stuff can kill you. Do I look reckless to you?"

They both smiled at that.

In that throaty purr, Nicole said, "What do you know about my husband?"

I shrugged. "United States senator from New York. Democrat but not crazy liberal. Rose through local ranks to the state legislature." I shifted my gaze toward Winters. "Formerly a NYC-based publicist for TV and movie people, a skill that comes in handy now that you're promoting yourself. And with the talk about a possible White House bid, your Hollywood connections will come in handy."

The dazzler smile again. "Do I have *your* vote, Mike?"

I shook my head. "My secretary says I'm just to the right of Attila the Hun. Not that winning me over matters. I haven't voted in years."

Nicole frowned in confusion. "Why not, Mike?"

I looked at her husband. "It only encourages them."

They were frozen for a couple of seconds, then burst into laughter.

"Mike," Winters said, "you strike me as someone who has his ear to the ground, in this town."

"I have my ins. With the cops. With the press boys. Uh, that's what broken-down P.I.'s like me call the media."

They were smiling. They seemed comfortable. And then they exchanged lingering glances that I couldn't quite read.

Finally Winters looked right at me, as if landing my vote might yet be possible, and said, "Okay, then. What *negative*s have you heard about me?"

"Other than that you're too damn liberal? Actually, some of my Democrat friends... and I do have some... think you're not liberal enough. That you ride the center lane and try to make everybody love you."

Winters said, "Is that so wrong?"

"No. Go for it. I mean, everybody loves *me*, and it's really great."

They laughed at that, too, gently. Which was about all it deserved.

"I take it," I said, "that there's something I *might* have known. Had my ear been even closer to the ground."

They again looked at each other, and Nicole pulled in a deep breath and let it out slow. Which was something to see.

Then she nodded and her husband turned to me and said, "There might be scuttlebutt about our private life. We've largely been discreet, but... well, sometimes it's hard to keep, uh..."

"The cat in the bag? Or should I say pussy?"

He swallowed and her eyebrows flicked up.

"Tell me," I said.

He swallowed. Let out a long sigh.

"Mike... Nicole and I love each other very much. We're devoted. And she's devoted to my career, too, and I support her in her causes, and—"

"Keep that up and I might puke all over this lovely new office.

It's a hard smell to get out. What smell are you hiding?"

They looked at each other again, blank stares that spoke volumes. Then they nodded at each other.

The senator said, "From the start of our marriage... even before that, when we realized we wanted to be together... we also wanted to be with other people. We have... healthy appetites."

"We have an open marriage," Nicole said bluntly.

"Open to you," I said, "closed to the public."

"There was a time," Winters said, gesturing off-handedly, "when the press looked the other way about such things. JFK and Marilyn and all that. But that time appears to be over."

"Yeah," I said. "Goes back to when Gary Hart suggested the press follow him around and see for themselves how he wasn't cheating... and as I recall, he didn't get to be president, did he?"

"Didn't even get to *try*," Winters said.

"You two will have to change your ways," I said, "if you're going for the big brass ring on the Pennsylvania Avenue merry-go-round. At least till you're out of office... then nobody will care, or anyway not so much."

He reached his hand out to her and she took it; they squeezed. "We know."

I shook a finger at them. "From here on out, you need to be the most faithful couple this side of Missionary Position, Montana."

They smiled a little. Nodded.

"But," I said, "somehow I don't think you called me here for marriage counseling."

Again, they exchanged glances.

"Blackmail?" I asked.

He nodded. Then she did the same.

"An anonymous male caller," Winters said, "is in possession of a tape recording of… of a sexual episode of mine."

I frowned. "Caller, you said. This was a phone call?"

"Yes."

"No idea who?"

"None."

"Any money demand yet?"

"'The price will follow,' he said."

With Vankemp money in the mix, that would be hefty.

I said, "Yet you're sure he has such a tape?"

Winters nodded glumly. "He played part of it for me, over the phone."

"Did you recognize the voices on the tape? I assume it was more than just slap-and-tickle that got recorded."

Nicole slipped her arm around her husband's shoulder. "Jamie and his secretary, Lisa Long, have in the last year or so had a sporadic… dalliance."

"And it was Lisa's voice on the tape?"

Again Winters nodded glumly. "And mine."

"Okay, does Lisa know about this open marriage of yours?"

Another exchange of looks.

But it was Nicole who answered. "No. I'm afraid she's in love with my husband. He intends to break it off, gently, and he believes… and I believe… he can do that. Of course, if Lisa has *sensed* something…"

I said, "She could be behind this. Or at least an accomplice."

Winters batted that way. "Impossible. She's a very moral girl. She wouldn't do any such thing."

"Like," I said, "she wouldn't fool around with a married man."

The wife's eyebrows went up. The husband's chin dropped down.

I stood. "I need the names of the women you've been with since you married Nicole. And I need all the information you can quickly put together on these women, including current addresses and phone numbers. You may have to pay some of them off."

"Oh," he said, "I can't imagine…"

"I can. Look, this is not my usual kind of job. I don't handle divorce work, for example. But I will do my best for you. Blackmailers piss me off. Please tell me you aren't involved in swinging, and that this catting around hasn't been with a dozen damn women."

"No swapping," he said, holding up a palm as if swearing in, in court. "Just three women. Not counting Lisa."

"So what do you want me to do, exactly?"

"What *can* you do?"

"Try to lay hands on that tape and any copies. Act as a go-between with the blackmailer and pay him off, at the same time making it clear any subsequent attempts for further payment will be dealt with harshly. Mike Hammer style."

They traded nodding looks.

The senator said, "How can you assure us confidentiality? Blackmail *is* a crime, after all."

"Yes, and a licensed private investigator is an officer of the court. But my contracts all go through an attorney. Technically you'll be his firm's client. That makes me a lawyer's leg man and protects you with attorney/client privilege."

They were openly smiling now.

Nicole asked, "Will a $10,000 retainer, non-refundable, do the trick?"

I grinned. "It'll stand up on its back legs and balance a ball on its nose. Based on $250 a day with my expenses covered."

Nicole, very efficient, said, "I'll gather those materials and have them for you… will tomorrow afternoon be soon enough? At your office?"

I said to him, "You should make *her* your secretary."

They were holding hands as I went out, the wind whipping at those plastic rectangles. The sheets fluttered like human flesh in a wind tunnel.

The gray sky rumbled more aggressively as I left the construction site, escorted by the chatty rumple-faced ex-cop in the security uniform. But the storm never came.

Not just then.

CHAPTER TWO

The next morning, a Wednesday, I filled Velda in on the Winters meeting and got her take on it.

Despite her secretary designation, she is first and foremost my partner in the private eye business. Her pre-MICHAEL HAMMER INVESTIGATIONS past includes a wartime stint with military intelligence and vice squad work on the NYPD— both before she was old enough to vote.

She packs a variety of deadly little revolvers and automatics, depending on which purse she selects for her day- or nighttime ensemble. Sometimes there's a sharp little knife in a sheath on the inside of a lovely thigh. She has custom-designed evening gowns with a slit up the front for easy access. To the sharp little knife, I mean.

Her ensemble that morning was nothing so exotic—a white silk blouse, a black pencil skirt, nylons, with low-riding black-and-white heels, her shoes the only real fashion touch at work. She doesn't wear much make-up—doesn't need to, though the candy-apple red of her lipstick carries quite a punch. She wears an engagement ring with a rock that would choke a horse, which tells you when I say she's my partner, I'm covering several bases. We haven't set the date yet. Let's not get ahead of ourselves—we've only been together since just after the war.

Let's get this out of the way. I am hovering around sixty—which side of that is my business—and Velda's only a little younger, though you would make her for no more than forty. She has hair in a timeless, shoulder-length pageboy style as black as Edgar Allan's raven and eyes so big and brown you can get lost in them. She is damn near as tall as me and built like Cyd Charisse and just as lovely.

"The Winters woman wore a black leather catsuit to a business meeting?" she asked, both eyebrows climbing.

She was sitting at her desk, opposite the entry of the office, which is roomy enough for a few reception chairs on either side and a table for coffee and snacks under a window. Behind her and to her right a little is the door to the inner office—my domain.

The Hackard Building had been around since the original Vankemp's day, but a while back it got a wholesale facelift. But we were still occupying the same eighth-floor space we'd been in forever, just spruced up and modernized some.

"Nicole Vankemp always did have a reputation," I said, "as a wild child."

"With a social conscience," Velda amended. "But she's married now, to a United States senator, with presidential ambitions. She'll have to change her ways. Or anyway her style."

I was sitting on half a hip on a corner of her desk, sipping coffee from the cup that says MIKE. I'm a cream-and-sugar guy. A real pansy.

"Maybe not," I said. "Times are changing."

She hiked just one eyebrow. "Not enough to get an open marriage past the Bible Belt."

"You're probably right about that. And you may see her and her hubby change their style as that White House try gathers steam. For the moment, it's enough to see if this blackmail thing can be quashed."

She was shaking her head, the long arcs of shimmering black swinging like pretty scythes. "If they pay the blackmailer off," she said, "they're only inviting another scandal."

I nodded. "Not to mention an ongoing payday for the extortionist."

She looked at me with eyes as wide as they were beautiful. "So what's your approach, Big Boy? Threaten the blackmailer? Rough him up and generally terrorize him?"

"There was a time," I admitted. "I think we start with getting that tape and destroying it."

"Even if you lay hands on it, how can you be sure there aren't copies?"

"That's when terrorizing the blackmailer becomes a real option."

The rest of the morning was spent on some insurance work, billing, and me dictating a few letters—the exciting fare that doesn't make it into these narratives but pays the bills. Business as usual, only Velda now had a personal computer and printer to work with. It wasn't till after our usual lunch at the deli down the street that Nicole Vankemp-Winters blew in.

No black leather catsuit today—but her slacks were just as tight and black, and her emerald double-breasted blazer with shoulder pads, over a lacy white blouse, hit the red of her hair like a slap. She had an oversize matching-color purse that *was* leather, slung over her shoulder on a strap. Her make-up was as heavy as Velda's wasn't, yet skillfully applied, from the turquoise eye shadow to the dark crimson lipstick.

She said, breathless, "Hope it's okay I drop in like this, Mike."

I was standing next to Velda's desk, handing her some field notes of mine to work up. For a moment Nicole seemed not to see Velda—which was sort of like Sophia Loren not noticing Gina Lollobrigida—but she remedied that by going straight to Velda with an outstretched hand.

The two beauties clasped pretty palms and Velda was soon smiling because Nicole was saying, "And you're the famous Velda! You've been in the news almost as much as your notorious boss. Your pictures don't do you justice—they're only gorgeous."

I don't figure Velda really bought that flattery, but she liked hearing it anyway, and appreciated the effort.

Like an operative reporting in, Nicole stood before Velda's desk and fished a handful of manila folders out of the big green leather purse.

"I know I really should have called and set a specific time," Nicole said to both of us. "But I've been running around gathering intel for you. That's the word, isn't it? Intel?"

"That's the word," I said.

The redhead held out the manila folders—three of them—and glanced from me to Velda and back again, not sure who to hand them to.

I took them and nodded toward the inner office door. "Let's

go into my sanctum sanctorum. Velda, your notebook? Nicole, would you like coffee? A soft drink?"

Our client smiled a little. "Not beer? You disappoint me, Mr. Hammer."

"We do have beer," I said with a grin, holding the door open for her, "and I'll be glad to fetch you one. There's a little fridge near my desk. But I've weaned myself off the stuff during business hours."

Her laugh was throaty, too. "No beer, thanks. But you're not living up to your reputation very well."

"I'll work at it harder."

Nicole went into my office and I watched the nice rear view, then glanced at Velda, already on her feet with her notepad and pencil poised, and giving me a look that said I had *better* not live up to my reputation....

I settled behind my desk. Nicole had already taken the client's chair. Velda sat behind Nicole and to one side, her legs crossed and reminding me how damn lucky I was.

Right now Velda was watching me close to see if I'd slip my hand under the desk to work the switch that starts the tape recorder in my bottom desk drawer. I shook my head just a little to signal I wouldn't be. Our clients had specifically asked for discretion and we'd give it to them.

Nicole got right to it. She handed me one of the three folders and hung onto the other two. She watched as I flipped it open.

An attractive brunette looked back at me, her hair short and permed, her features pretty if not distinctive; in business attire, she sat at a desk, posing for a photo suitable for an employee publication or company roster.

"That's Helen Wayne," Nicole said. "Jamie's secretary."

I frowned, photo in hand. "I thought Lisa Long was your husband's secretary."

"Lisa is his current secretary. The Wayne woman worked for him for two years and a few months. She left in March and the Long woman took over the position."

Probably multiple positions.

I asked, "Has that been a habit with Mr. Winters? Affairs with secretaries?"

"No," she said. Nothing defensive in her tone. If she cared about him cheating, she didn't show it.

I looked over what had been written up. It was a dispassionate report—material culled from employment records.

I asked, "You wrote and typed this yourself?"

"I did. Well, I use a word processor."

"This information came from your husband's files? The job application she filled out, annual employee evaluations and so on?"

She nodded, the red hair bouncing. "And I asked Jamie what he knew about her."

Her attitude seemed damn near clinical.

I returned my attention to the folder.

Helen Wayne was from Granville, Ohio. She attended Antioch College. Took business. Went to New York and got a job as secretary to Senator Winters in the office he maintained in Manhattan when he wasn't in Washington, D.C. It had been her first job. Her work record, in the senator's employ, was stellar.

Since leaving, she was taking graduate courses at NYU, studying to be a legal secretary, working part-time as a clerk in a bookstore in the East Village, where she lived. She and the senator had broken their relationship off amicably and had not been in touch since.

I handed the folder out for Velda. She got up, took it, and returned to her chair.

As Velda perused the pages, I said to Nicole, "You consider yours an open marriage."

It wasn't exactly a question.

Nicole flicked a look at Velda, engrossed in the folder, then her eyes went to me with unspoken worry.

I answered it: "Miss Sterling… that's Velda… has been briefed on everything you and your husband shared with me last night. We are a two-person firm and have no secrets from each other. My apologies if I should have made that clear."

She raised a palm. "No, no… that's fine. You were saying?"

"This open marriage of yours and your husband's. That implies… really, more than implies… that you are not faithful to Jamie in the traditional sense."

She took that just fine. "We are faithful," Nicole said, "in that we *too* have no secrets." She threw a little smile in Velda's direction, without turning to her, Velda still absorbed in her reading.

I said, "Your list of extracurricular encounters… is it similar to Jamie's? Counting Lisa Long, we're talking four playmates. What is your…" I searched for a word.

"Box score?" Nicole asked, impishly.

Velda caught that, looking up with an open-mouthed smile.

"Considerably higher," Nicole said. "I go clubbing on my own. I have many friends. No stranger at cocktail parties and fund-raisers, attend Broadway openings." She shrugged elaborately. "Jamie isn't any more jealous than I am. We just follow different paths."

"In what sense?"

She shrugged, the red mane bouncing once. "He has his little flings. Affairs. Relationships. I'm more a… one-night stand kind of girl. My man is my man. *That's* the relationship in my life. The rest are just…" Now *she* looked for a word.

Velda offered, "The spice of life."

Nicole smiled back at her. "Yes. Precisely." She spoke to us both, looking back and forth. "I am not careless. In the current climate, I take precautions. Safe sex only."

Velda asked, "Does that go for the senator as well?"

"Very much so. We tell each other about our various adventures. Laugh. Excite each other with our… reports back to the home front."

Velda gave me a wide-eyed look.

"You mentioned clubbing," I said to Nicole. "Those are notorious venues for illegal narcotics."

Nicole shook her head; every time she did that, the red hair got more tousled and sexy, as if somebody like Vidal Sassoon had just touched her up.

She said, "Never my thing, the consciousness-expanding bit. Not even grass. Recreational drugs are of no interest to me. I like to feel *in* control. And before you ask… I have put all that behind me. The discos, that is. The parties. As we discussed last night, Jamie and I are a married couple and our sexual activities will henceforth be confined to ye olde marital bed."

I nodded. "Good to hear. But what about blackmail from that side of your life? That side of your *night* life?"

"It could happen," she admitted. "But I am a known quantity.

In my modest way, I am famous. My sins will be forgiven where my husband's would not. Particularly if I become a one-man gal."

Velda smiled at that, then asked, "Were any of your casual liaisons with individuals who might have deeper feelings for you than you intended to, uh… stir?"

The red mane shook again. "Very doubtful… if by that you mean the blackmailer plaguing Jamie and me might be some bitter ex-lover. As I said, I was never into prolonged affairs."

"Just the same," I said, "you should give us a rundown on your sexual partners, specifically those since you became the wife of a senator."

She nodded. "Understood. Something like what I've given you today on Jamie's playthings?"

"Yes," I said. "If that doesn't require writing *War and Peace*."

She smirked. "How are you spelling that?"

Everyone laughed a little.

Then we went over the other two folders.

Judith McGuire—Judy—had been a campaign worker of the senator's. That was a relationship that began before Nicole and Jamie got married, and continued for several months thereafter.

A pretty little blonde, caught in a snapshot at campaign HQ, Judy was an admirer of the senator and never had any stated designs on him beyond the fun and excitement of being desired by such an important man. (Whose words those were—Judy's or Jamie's or Nicole's—I didn't know and didn't ask.)

She was from upstate New York, had gone to a community college for two years, and was now at NYU. She too was living in Greenwich Village, and worked as a waitress.

The third young woman on the senator's to-do list was Nora Kent, who also lived in the Village. Was that a coincidence or something significant? I filed that thought away. For now, I knew she was an old-fashioned cabaret singer who had a regular gig at a piano bar on Grove Street. She was from the Bronx and had taken jazz studies at Julliard.

The folders provided current addresses and phone numbers for all three women.

Velda, finishing up her look at the third folder, asked, "Should I phone them?"

I thought for a moment, then said, "No. Make in-person cold calls. Start out saying you're an investigator working with a *Daily News* reporter on rumors of extramarital affairs involving the senator."

"What?" Nicole blurted.

I held up a hand. Continued giving Velda her instructions.

"Get their reactions. Get your own read on each. Then tell them the truth—that we're really working for the senator, and he's being blackmailed over his sexual indiscretions. Nothing about the tape with the Long woman, though."

Velda, sitting forward on her chair, the folders in her lap, said to Nicole, "Lisa Long still works for your husband, as his secretary?"

"Yes."

"You didn't work up a folder on her?"

Nicole shook her head and all that red hair came along for a ride. "No—I can if you like, but you should be able to get anything you need directly from her."

I said, "She doesn't know about the blackmail threat?"

Nicole shrugged. "I wasn't sure we'd want to involve her."

Velda goggled at me, and I said to our client, "I'd say she's already involved."

The redhead didn't seem concerned. "Whatever you think is best."

Velda sat forward. "Mike, should I talk to her?"

"No," I said. "I'll handle that."

Velda nodded, stood, and tucked the folders under her arm. "I think I should get started."

I said I thought so, too.

The two women exchanged their nice-to-meet-yous and goodbyes, and then Velda was gone and I was alone with my client. Or anyway one of my two clients on this job.

"Quite a woman," Nicole said, raising an eyebrow in much the same fashion Velda was prone to.

"No argument."

She was slowly nodding. "Now it's clear to me."

"What is?"

Nicole rose and shut the inner office door, then came over and perched on a corner of my desk. Like I had perched on Velda's desk, earlier. She looked down at me with a cat-that-ate-the-canary smile.

She said, "I understand why you took Jamie and me on. Part of why, anyhow. Why you didn't disapprove of our ways. I mean, you have your own code of morality, and not everybody fits it."

"You lost me."

"I don't think so." She touched the tip of my nose with an orange-red-nailed finger, very lightly. "I'll be honest with you. I did hear about you two. Velda something and Mike Hammer."

"You did, huh? Not on the society page."

Nicole shrugged, worked up an impish smile. "Another part of the paper. Cindy Adams. Liz Smith."

She slipped off the desk and came around and sat in my lap and put her arms around my neck. "You could identify with us. Because you two have an open relationship, too."

I started to say something, but she leaned in and kissed my mouth, a lipsticky kiss, warm, almost hot; it lasted a while, as she tasted me, then she flicked her tongue into my mouth, just a snake's flick.

"If I have to behave, from now on," she said, "I'm going to have to cultivate a few good friends I can trust."

"I'm a little old for you, aren't I, doll?"

"Doll! Such ancient words come out of you, Mike. No, I like the idea of an older man. A man who's experienced things I haven't. Who's killed. Who's loved. Who knows how to be... discreet." She ground herself into my lap. "And I can *tell* you're interested."

"Hell, baby, I'm old. I'm not dead."

She kissed me again. Not a big deal this time. Just a friendly follow-up. A period on the end of a very sexy sentence.

"You got the tense wrong," I said. "Earlier?"

"What tense?"

"It's 'had' an open relationship. Velda and me. We had one for a lot of years."

"Did you now?"

"Yeah. But it was one-sided."

The green eyes flared. "Ah! You were a *tomcat* while she was a faithful feline."

"Something like that."

"So what closed it? Your open relationship."

I shrugged. "I got tired of being an asshole."

She ground her rump some more. "How's that working out?"

Without leaving my chair, I picked her up by the waist and stood her on the floor.

"It's working out fine," I said.

Running fingers through some of that red mane, she nodded toward my lap and the contrary evidence. "Are you *sure*, Mike?"

"Damn sure."

Nicole shrugged and headed for the door. "Your loss."

She was halfway out when I gave her the kicker.

"See, I'm still an asshole," I said. "Just a one-woman asshole now."

CHAPTER THREE

Until he made the move into his new digs elsewhere on Park Avenue, Senator Jamie Winters would be maintaining his office on the nineteenth floor of the Flatiron Building.

And the Flatiron is where I headed, mid-afternoon, catching a cab outside the Hackard Building. When traffic got tight, I paid the hackie, climbed out and walked the last few blocks. No trenchcoat today, just a gray Perry Ellis suit Velda steered me toward, with a gray-and-black striped tie I selected myself; but for all those efforts, the porkpie fedora still branded me a relic.

The day was cool and crisp but sunny, and up ahead I could see Madison Square Park, moms and kids here for the playground and people walking their dogs amid the mix of evergreens and fiery fall browns, reds, yellows and oranges. Nobody looked like they had blackmail in their life, or a private detective on retainer, either.

In Thadeous Vankemp's heyday, the Flatiron Building—that triangular structure on its triangular lot bordered by Broadway, Fifth Avenue and East 22nd Street—had been one of the tallest buildings in Manhattan. Now it was officially an historic landmark, twenty-two stories dwarfed by towering neighbors, its distinctive

Beaux-Arts design, in a shape reminiscent of an old-fashioned cast-iron clothes iron, still setting it apart.

The Flatiron lobby was, not surprisingly, narrow—a beige, art-deco, marble-floored space with framed pictures detailing the building's history. Tourists couldn't get past the guard at his desk, but I was expected. I took the elevator to the nineteenth floor, to the office where the senator met with everybody from lowly constituents to NYC power brokers.

I already knew Jamie Winters wasn't in—but I wasn't calling on him.

In the senator's outer office, blandly modern walls at left and right slanted inward as if presenting the young woman behind the reception desk—*tah dah!* You'd think she was something special.

You'd be right.

Lisa Long was the only one of Jamie's paramours whose picture and background I had not been given. Yet I had no doubt I was standing before the most recent object of the senator's affections.

She wore a white no-nonsense blouse under a black suit with shoulder pads and a white pocket hanky, plus minimal but well-chosen jewelry by way of hoop earrings and oversized bracelets. Her big brunette mane, not unlike the red one her lover's wife sported, was offset by heavy dark-framed oversize eyeglasses that tried to overwhelm the lovely face, but couldn't. From behind them, big brown eyes with dark thick eyebrows courtesy of Brooke Shields looked at me coolly, her high cheekbones rouged, her sensuous mouth home to coral gloss lipstick and a slight, business-like smile.

Still, I asked, from the doorway: "Miss Long? Mike Hammer. I believe you're expecting me."

Her smile warmed up a little. "Yes, Mr. Hammer," she said in a nice second soprano, waving me in gently. "Mrs. Winters called and said you'd be stopping by with a few questions."

As I approached, she gestured to the black metal chair in front of her L-shaped desk; to her right loomed a workstation with massive computer set-up—terminal, monitor, keyboard and printer. I took off my hat, which I set on the uncluttered half of the desk, where a phone with combination intercom and answer machine, a pen and pencil holder, a notepad and a stapler were about it.

"I understand you're a private investigator," she said.

In her mid-twenties, she was unlikely to have encountered the wilder exploits of my younger days, even if her folks read the tabloids.

"Yes, I am," I admitted. "Working for both Mrs. Winters and the senator."

The secretary tented her fingers; her nails were coral too, well manicured and not long—with that computer keyboard, long nails wouldn't have been practical.

She said, "I was told to give you full cooperation, and access to the senator's office, including his files if necessary. But nothing of what this is about."

"The subject is a delicate one," I said, "but the senator himself assured me of your discretion."

She nodded, the eyes behind the big lenses half-closing, as she tried to process that. "Of course. How can I be of help?"

I grinned, not too big, crossed my legs, gestured around us. "Doesn't exactly seem to be hopping around here."

She smiled, not big at all. "There are days. Right now, there's nothing major on the senator's political agenda."

"If something big is pending, voters drop by in person?"

She nodded, still smiling a little.

"And lobbyists and so on."

She shrugged, the shoulder pads making it seem bigger than it was. "Most of that happens in D.C. We do hear from all sorts of constituents, from locals with their special problems to... well, giants of business and industry, who want the senator's ear, personally."

"You must meet some very important people."

The smile grew a bit. "Yes. In passing."

I folded my arms and leaned back in a chair not designed to encourage long visits. "The senator is lucky to have such a pleasant presence guarding the gate. What's your story, Miss Long?"

That question surprised her and she batted long lashes that seemed to be real, if heavy with mascara. "Excuse me?"

"Part of what I'm doing is gathering background material. Where you're from, where you went to school, and so on."

She thought that over, and then gave me a just-the-facts recital. She was from Bayonne, New Jersey. Her father was a fireman there, her mother a housewife; she had a younger sister and older brother. She had gone to Middlesex County College in Edison, where she studied to be an administrative assistant and took "secretarial science."

I asked, "That's a two-year degree?"

"Yes."

"Working-class girl, then."

She bristled just a little. "That's right."

I held up a palm. "Hey, I'm a junior college grad myself. Took a while. Nights. Police science. We're a couple of scientists, looks like."

She unbristled and decided to smile again. "What did *your* father do, Mr. Hammer?"

"Bartender. So do you travel to D.C. with the senator? Run his office there?"

She shook her head, the bounce of that stylish thatch of hers reminding me of Nicole again. Why did men so often have affairs with women who looked like their wives? If you're tired of Coke, why have a Pepsi?

"I hold down the New York office," she said, cocking her head. "He has a considerable staff in Washington… You're not writing anything down."

"I'm getting what I need, Ms. Long. When did your involvement with the senator begin?"

She blinked, then the big brown eyes stayed open wide. "Excuse me?"

"The senator wasn't specific. How long, as they say, has this been going on? Couldn't be *too* long, because I don't make you for over twenty-five or -six."

She swallowed. "I don't think there's any reason for…"

For what she didn't seem able to say.

"Mrs. Winters told you to give me full cooperation," I reminded her. "She's aware of the affair, and the senator is aware that *she's* aware."

This cool, professional young woman seemed clearly flustered now. "You've been misinformed, Mr., what was it?"

"Hammer."

"Mr. Hammer." She smoothed the front of her. Did I mention she had a nice figure? She had a nice figure.

She went on: "There is no affair. My relationship with the senator is strictly employer/employee."

I'd run into a lot of those in my time.

I sat there smirking, a conscious prick move, and let her spin her wheels: "Mr. Hammer, I think Mrs. Winters may have some unfounded suspicions, and has sold you a bill of goods. I have no... intimate relationship with Senator Winters. I can't imagine him confirming this outrageous assertion. Surely you haven't talked to him directly."

I shook my head slowly. "I'm afraid I have, Ms. Long. I met with both the senator and his wife, at the same time. And your relationship with him... your 'intimate relationship'... is not his first affair."

I almost said "dalliance," but figured that might insult her, not wanting to push the prick thing too far.

Her chin came up and the lids on the eyes came back down, to half-mast. "I suppose that's possible," she said, some ice hanging on the words. "The senator's marriage is a most unhappy one." The chin came up even further. "His wife has been cheating on *him* for years."

Imagine that.

"If this..." Her voice tried to be strong—it was certainly louder now—but a quaver gave her away. "...if this is... something that woman has initiated... if that's the kind of investigator *you* are..."

I held up a hand. "I don't do divorce work. This is more serious than that."

She laughed humorlessly, then huffed, "More serious than *divorce?*"

"The senator is being blackmailed."

Now she had no expression at all. Just wide-open eyes. Then she said, "Oh dear."

I was careful not to say that she was part of that. But I was bum enough to at least vaguely suggest she might be.

Holding up a hand again, I said, "As I say, the senator's had a lot of relationships over the years. It's somewhat surprising he's not had the press dogging his heels on that account during previous campaigns. Or that he hasn't encountered blackmail before, although perhaps he has. I wouldn't necessarily know. This is my first job for Mr. and Mrs. Winters."

That was kind of cruel—saying "Mr. and Mrs. Winters." She seemed to shrink in her chair.

Then, in a very small voice, reminding me how recently she'd been a little girl, the young woman asked, "What can I do? To help. Help make this go away. Is Jamie… is Jamie going to pay whoever this is?"

Calling him Jamie dropped any last hint of denial from the senator's latest mistress.

I said, "I really don't know. I hope to find the person responsible and stop them."

"And take them to the police?"

"No. Hell no."

She sat forward. "What *can* you do, Mr. Hammer?"

"You say your father is a fireman in New Jersey? He's still alive?"

"Very much so. He's still on the job."

I got a little melodramatic then. I unbuttoned the Perry Ellis jacket and let her glimpse the massive-looking butt of the .45 Colt Automatic, U.S. Army model, vintage 1914, in the shoulder sling, which had required some tailoring.

I said to the young woman, who was vintage 1966 or so, "Ask your old man who Mike Hammer is."

She took that in, swallowed, nodded.

I asked, "Who knows about the affair?"

She frowned, not angry, more surprised. "Well, *no one*, of course!"

"A roommate?"

"No. No, no."

"Do you *have* a roommate?"

"No, not since…"

"Since the senator got you your own place?"

"How did you know that?"

"I'm a detective. No girlfriends who know?"

"No girlfriends who know, no."

"Now, Ms. Long… Lisa… if you have a boyfriend on the side…" That sounded funny—a mistress with a boyfriend on the side—but it was all too typical. "…you need to tell me."

"No!"

"No, you won't tell me?"

"No, I don't have a boyfriend! On the side or anywhere."

"Other than the senator, you mean."

"…Other than the senator."

"Because if you do," I said, and buttoned the coat back up, "I'll find out. Again, ask your old man."

She swallowed. "I don't have a boyfriend."

"Well, if you do, young lady," I said, putting some condescension in, "and you two are in on this together? You should tell me now. And I'll put an end to this with nobody getting hurt or going to jail. I promise you that."

Halfway through that little speech, she began shaking her head—*no, no, no!*—and got all that brown stuff tousled. She started to cry and her make-up ran. She got a box of tissues out of a drawer and tried to clean herself up. It wasn't enough.

She rose unsteadily. "Mr. Hammer... I need to use the rest room...."

I stood. "I'm going to have a look at the senator's inner office while you do that. Okay? It's unlocked?"

She nodded, swallowed, obviously appreciating the opportunity to freshen up, and hurried out.

At least she was on one of the odd-numbered floors. When this place was built, there were only men's rooms. Now it was MEN on the even and WOMEN on the odd. Finally some equality.

As had been the case with the unfinished office in the high-rise-in-progress, a mahogany door announced SENATOR JAMIE B. WINTERS with a nameplate. As promised, the door wasn't locked, but the other side of that door revealed it could be locked from within, turning the workplace into a trysting spot.

I was in the front prow of the building now, a space filled with light even mid-afternoon. The walls narrowed to six feet across, where a curved balcony faced north onto the park, and from here you could get a good look at two large Corinthian columns and the top of a terra-cotta medallion.

The walls were eggshell white, the one at my left arrayed with framed photos of the senator with other famous people—photos signed by the various celebs to him. Michael Jackson, Whitney Houston, Bill Cosby and other movie and music luminaries, were joined by President Carter, Walter Mondale, and Teddy Kennedy, plus sports figures including George Steinbrenner, Joe Namath, and O.J. Simpson. These hung above several old-fashioned radiators, which were putting out just enough heat to deal with the fall cold snap.

On the right was a very comfortable-looking brown leather couch. I gave it a raised-eyebrow look, just in case it was in the mood to make a confession. It wasn't talking, but it did whisper. Two file cabinets faced each other just beyond the couch, their sides to the wall, to deal with the narrowing space.

The senator's desk was at right, too, the back of it to the wall with a visitor's chair along the right-hand side. Winters would have to swivel a little to give a guest proper attention. Claustrophobic as it was in here, this remained an impressive office, truly one of a kind—or one of a handful, since there were potentially another twenty or so spaces like this elsewhere in the building.

I didn't bother with the file cabinets. I doubted the senator kept folders on his conquests, and anyway I had the ones his wife had worked up, right? But the drawers to his mahogany desk were worth a look. I expected they might be locked, one or two of them anyway, but that wasn't the case. And the drawer on the bottom right was a pip.

It was home to a "value" box of Trojan rubbers, a few sex toys and several bottles of booze—whiskey and vodka. I'd already spied a little fridge on the other side of the desk. Did I really have to check it for ice and mixer?

By the time I was through in the inner office, the senator's secretary was back at her desk, looking like a million bucks again. I thought, *Some guys have all the luck*, then remembered who my secretary had been for a lot of years now. And this little doll probably couldn't even handle a gun.

"You all right?" I asked her, standing by her desk.

"Yes, thank you."

"You look fine."

"Thank you."

"I didn't mean to upset you, but I'm that guy you hear about who goes around doing all those dirty jobs that somebody has to do."

That made her smile a little. "How can I help?"

"You've helped plenty already." I noticed the intercom/answer machine on the desk. "Let me try something."

"Pardon?"

I handed her the receiver and hit record on the machine, then said, "I'm going back in the senator's office. Call me on the intercom."

She frowned in confusion. "Okay…"

I went in there and then her voice came over the little tinny mate to the intercom on her desk. "Can you hear me, Mr. Hammer?"

"Yeah. I can hear you fine, Ms. Long. Leave the connection open till I say otherwise."

"Yes, sir."

That was the problem, being my age. Women who looked like her always called men who looked like me "sir."

I went over to the couch and sat, then spoke in a normal tone. "This is a test. Testing, one two three."

Then I got up and went all the way down to where the prow-shaped office was only six feet wide. In a normal voice, I said, "This is Mike Hammer. You're a very lovely young woman, in case I forgot to mention it."

Then I went over by the desk and said to the intercom, "Okay, Ms. Long. Shut 'er off."

I walked back into the outer office where a red light was flashing on the answer machine. I hit play. It rewound automatically, and then I heard everything I'd said in the inner office, including how lovely Ms. Long was.

She looked up at me like I'd just invented the light bulb. I smiled down at her and she smiled back at me till her smile soured. She'd just figured it out.

Any hanky-panky going on in that inner office could be recorded by somebody out here.

She covered her mouth with those coral-tipped fingers, and her eyes were so huge the big lenses barely contained them.

"Someone..." she began. "Someone has a tape of... of the senator and I...?"

"Yeah. May I assume you reserved your socializing till after office hours?"

She nodded, nodded, nodded.

"Who could have been in the building when you two were occupied?"

"We always went out for dinner first. Sometimes to a show, movie, play, you know. Then back here or to my apartment."

"I'm interested in when you were here, together. Who else would be in the building then?"

That took no thought. "It was usually pretty late. A security guard, doing rounds. A cleaning woman."

"You know them? Know their names?"

"I know their *first* names. He's Myron and she's Erin. She lives in Brooklyn, I think, no older than me. You can probably get their names from the building superintendent."

I put a hand on her shoulder. "Okay. You just go on about your business as usual. I don't want you to worry."

"It'll be hard not to."

"You ask your father, the fireman."

"Ask him what?"

"Ask him if Mike Hammer will look out for you."

That seemed to reassure her for a moment, but as I went out, I glanced at her and she was hugging her arms to herself, shivering.

And it wasn't cold in there at all.

CHAPTER FOUR

When it opened back in '73, the new NYPD HQ, replacing the old Centre Street building, was described as a prime example of Brutalist architecture. Which is a fancy way of saying One Police Plaza, near City Hall and the Brooklyn Bridge, had all the personality of a big corrugated concrete box.

I had never gotten used to Captain Pat Chambers of Homicide working out of a glassed-in, modern, personality-free office off the bullpen's sea of metal desks and computers with their bulky monitors. Pat just never seemed to fit outside the world of scarred-up wooden desks and matching battered file cabinets, and certainly wasn't suited to being on fishbowl display at all times.

How's a guy supposed to slap an uncooperative suspect?

But he had brought his old brown leather swivel chair along with him, though the visitor's chair I settled myself into had a padded back and seat, to offset its Brutalist design. I felt damn near welcome.

"So what's this about?" he asked, narrowing the gray-blue eyes at me.

His tie was loose and he was in his rolled-up shirtsleeves. About my age, he had been my best friend since we'd gone to the police academy together, two lifetimes ago—a big, blond guy with no fat on him, and a still-handsome mug despite all the lines it had earned.

"It's just a job I'm on," I said. "I could use a little help, is all."

Suspicion was in his DNA. "What kind of help?"

"Just some background on a guy who used to be a cop."

He thought about that. "I heard somewhere you're a detective. That would seem like the sort of thing you could root out for yourself."

I grinned. "Do I have to give you the taxpayer speech?"

That got me a grin for my trouble. "Let's go back to my first question. What's this about?"

"Pat, it's just a job I'm on."

"I need some context."

"I can't give you any without betraying a client. Let's just say I'm looking into a security guy at a building where somebody may have entered my client's office with illegal intent."

No grin now. "Sounds like police business."

I shrugged, flipped a hand over. "It's just something I'm checking out. I have an address for this guy in the Bronx. But I thought maybe you might be familiar with him or know somebody who would be. The super I talked to said the guy retired from the detective bureau a couple of years ago, which might put him on your radar."

He rocked a little in the chair. "Security guy where?"

"Flatiron Building."

"What's the guy's name?"

"Myron Henry."

Pat stopped rocking. He leaned forward, folded his hands and looked at me like a warden regarding a prisoner who'd started more than his share of riots.

"You're kidding," he said.

"Yeah, this is a gag. A real rib-tickler. What the hell, Pat? What's the score on this Henry character?"

"You don't know?"

I threw my hands up. "Sure, I know all about him. I just wanted to waste your time. I get a charge out of that."

He cocked his head and gave me the wary look. "You must have smelled something or you would've just phoned. You dropped by 'cause you *heard* something."

I copped to it. "The name Myron Henry rang a bell, when the Flatiron building manager gave it to me. Something about pilfering. But all I remember is you making a passing comment, one time. Nothing that made the papers."

"Pilfering puts it mildly," Pat said, eyebrows up then down. "Henry was working Homicide, out in the Bronx, where he lives. Funny how every corpse he came across had no money on them."

"Not even pennies on their eyes, huh?"

Pat grunted a laugh, pointed out at the bullpen beyond the glass. "We moved him here, to burglary. Which I said was a mistake, because it muddied up whether the actual robberies hadn't been padded out by what Henry may have lifted."

"Was he ever brought up on charges?"

Pat shook his head. "Cops have a bad habit of staying loyal to each other, even when it's not deserved. Just like the bad guys, the good guys don't rat each other out."

"Even when one of theirs is a bad guy himself," I said, nodding. "But how could Henry have gotten on at the Flatiron, with that rep? Surely they checked his background."

"No charges, remember? File was clean. He even had a couple of commendations. But I knew what he was up to, and I called him on it."

"Even though he wasn't one of yours?"

Pat shrugged. "He'd got back on Homicide by then. This was just a couple of years ago."

"I don't remember running into him."

"Well, you've kept your nose out of my business lately, pretty much. How long has it been since you got wrapped up in a murder case?"

"That Penta business," I said, referring to a contract killer who'd targeted me last year. Guess who came out on top. "And before that, nothing much for damn near a decade."

"Face it, Mike. You're getting old."

"And you're getting younger? You gonna make inspector before you put yourself out to pasture or what?"

He smiled a little. "If you stay put on the bench, I just might. There are those who say my friendship with you has stood in my way, you know. How many self-defense pleas have you pulled off over the years?"

"Who's counting? Anyway, half of those framed commendations and medals on your wall over there are from cases I cracked and handed your way. So don't blame me for your lack of upward mobility. I've *seen* how you talk to the brass. Nobody takes less shit than Pat Chambers."

Now he grinned big. "Nobody but Mike Hammer."

"Sure, but I'm self-employed."

His expression darkened with thought. "Speaking of put-out-to-pasture... just between us insubordinate types, that's how I got rid of Henry. I led him to believe he'd be brought up on charges if he didn't take retirement at twenty years."

"Were you bluffing?"

Pat's eyes flared. "Hell yes! But Henry knew he'd made an enemy out of me and, even if he figured I didn't have the goods on him, he was smart enough to know I'd make him my hobby."

I nodded slowly. "Good to know."

Pat studied me. "So, Mike. What's this *really* about?"

I raised a palm. "No can do, buddy. Client confidentiality. But if things drift into your domain, I will let you know."

"Doesn't sound like murder." He chuckled, shook his head. "Kind of refreshing, seeing you tackle a real job, and not just goin' off on a tear, getting even with some poor bastard who had the nerve to screw over one of your friends."

"It does pay better," I admitted. "You want to do me another favor?"

"Do I have a choice?"

"Does Henry still have pals on the department? Somebody who might know his hangouts?"

Pat frowned, nodded, reached for the phone, punched an extension in, muttering, "Thank God not all the taxpayers want your kind of service... Donnigan, you must be about ready to head home for the day.... Glad I caught you. Stop by my office for a second."

He hung up and said, "You know Lou Donnigan, don't you, Mike?"

"Sure. Good man."

"He was Henry's partner, at the end. They got along."

Donnigan, a tall skinny plainclothes detective, was coming up the aisle between the rows of metal desks and cops writing reports and taking calls. A raincoat was over his arm. Pat nodded to him through the glass and they exchanged smiles and Donnigan opened the office door without knocking.

He leaned in, said, "What can I do you for, Captain?" Around forty, he had a homely, pockmarked face and thinning dirty blond hair, his light blue eyes and ready smile improving the mix.

"You know Mike Hammer," Pat said.

Donnigan grinned as I half-stood, and came all the way in to shake my hand. "Good to see you, Mike. Marry that good-looking secretary yet?"

"We're engaged," I said.

"Don't know what she sees in you."

"Nobody does."

I told Donnigan I was looking to connect with Myron Henry, and sooner was better than later. Any haunts of his ex-partner's where I might check? I'd already called his home in the Bronx and got no answer.

"Well," Donnigan said, "he's working security at the Flatiron, nights. I'm not telling tales out of school when I say he almost always stops for a few beers before he goes into work, and maybe grabs a sandwich. You know the Old Town Bar, there in the Flatiron district?"

I did. Most New Yorkers did.

Donnigan shrugged. "That's his home away from home."

"He strictly night shift?"

"Last I heard. Works four days a week, Tuesday through Friday, eight p.m. till six a.m."

From the Flatiron building manager, I'd got the name and other info of the Saturday-through-Monday guy, but Lisa Long said the senator's office was only open Tuesday through Friday.

I asked, "What can you tell me about your old partner, Lou?"

He shrugged. "I always liked him well enough. I never personally saw him exercise any sticky fingers, but of course I heard the scuttlebutt. We're not as tight as we were, though."

"Why's that?"

The homely face really could work up a nice smile. "Well, our wives were friendly, but he got divorced last year. His kids are grown and the missus threw him out. Can't blame her."

"Why's that?"

"He's a cheater. Those sticky fingers extend to more than just crime scenes and evidence lockers, I guess.... Anything else, Mike? Captain?"

No.

That was quite enough.

The sign, red on top and bottom, green in the middle, said

OLD TOWN

BAR

RESTAURANT

and must have gone back to at least the '40s. But the watering hole itself dated to 1892, and if it was ever remodeled, must have been before I was born.

The joint was proudly dark, dingy and narrow, with a long marble and mahogany bar with an endless bottle-lined mirror behind, sixteen-foot tin ceilings, and a subway-tile floor. The wooden booths sported well-worn green leather backing, and the white-shirt, black-tie bartenders were as efficient as they were surly.

Early evening the joint was pretty busy, a combo of people hanging out after work and others meeting up for a night out. For those in their twenties and thirties, this was just the first stop, but the regulars, age forty to the grave, were here for the duration. The dining room was upstairs and a dumbwaiter brought food from the basement, which wasn't an appetizing thought. But I settled into one of the booths and ordered a burger and fries, anyway, figuring the alcohol content of the Miller Lite would sterilize any germs.

I'd polished away the food, which was easily worth a third of what it cost, and was on my third beer when I started to wonder if he wasn't going to show.

Then he did.

I didn't know the guy, but I recognized him at once—Myron Henry had ex-cop written all over him. He was about five ten, pale as death, pushing fifty but looking solid, his bucket head home to a Marine-style haircut in a stylish salt-and-pepper shade, with a jutting jaw that could have used a Kirk Douglas dimple. His expression was pleasant and his dark little close-set eyes crowded his hawkish nose, making him look kind of stupid.

That probably gave him an edge.

And if you're wondering how I could be so confident that this was my guy and an ex-cop, it's not because I'm the greatest detective in the world: he was wearing a dark blue shirt and lighter blue pants and a security guard badge. If he carried a gun and/ or a baton on the job, they must be in his locker at the Flatiron.

He was about to slide onto a stool when I called out from my nearby booth: "Hey, Myron!"

He turned and squinted at me with those dark eyes that looked dumb but weren't. He came over slow, thinking all the way.

"You're Mike Hammer," he said.

"Yeah. You used to work burglary. Sit down. I'll buy you one."

He thought about that, shrugged, looked at a bartender, which was how a regular ordered in a place like this, and then sat across from me in the ancient wooden booth. The jukebox was playing Sinatra's "New York, New York." Sue me.

"I don't remember," Myron Henry said, "we ever met."

"I don't think we ever did. You were pointed out to me, though." Not true.

"What? By your pal, Chambers?"

I smiled a little. Sipped some Miller. "Well, Pat can be that way."

"What way?"

"Kind of a stickler, sometimes. Can be a real tight-ass, you know?"

He shrugged, hunkered over. "What he is is a prick."

I turned the smile into a grin. "What, none of your pals are pricks?"

That got a grin out of him. A big-hair, lipstick-pout waitress came over, and he gave her a lecherous grin as she sat down a Pilsner of something on tap and summoned a smile for him, before carting off her nice fanny.

He sipped the beer I'd be paying for. Said, "You just bein' friendly, Hammer? One ex-cop to another? You *are* an ex-cop, right? What, you were on the job six months before they fired you?"

"About that long. But like the man says, they didn't fire me, I quit. They'd stuck me on a desk because I got carried away sometimes, on the street."

"You really as tough as they say?"

I shrugged. "Not anymore. Shit, I'm older than dirt. I brought frankincense to the Jesus baby. Or was it myrrh?"

He was giving me a hard look. "You seem like you're in shape, for an old fart."

"Yeah, I work out regular at Bing's. When you have a rep like mine, sometimes people get ideas."

"Even now?"

"Even now. Sometimes I have to give out a free lesson. You work at the Flatiron, I hear."

"That's right." The dark little eyes were suspicious, but they didn't narrow. They bore in. "Is *that* what this is about?"

"I'm not sure. What are *you* talking about?"

The eyes got even smaller. "When somebody like you turns up, I get to wondering—has somebody accused me of somethin'? Look, man, if there's been anything taken at the Flatiron, *I'm* not the one. You talk to the weekend guy. I don't do that shit no more."

"What shit?"

He finished the beer in a bunch of gulps, then looked at the bartender again. This was going to cost me at least two beers.

Myron Henry said, "I'm not saying I ever took a goddamn thing on the job, not from evidence or a crime scene neither. So if you're wearing a fuckin' wire for that pal of yours, guess again, tough guy. This ain't gonna play. And *I* work out, too, Hammer. I *have* to stay fit. You know how many floors I got to cover in an eight-hour shift? I work my tail off. So if something's missing, you talk to the *other* guy. The one on weekends."

"Nothing's missing, Myron. I'm not wearing a wire, either."

He held up both palms. "Well, if you *are*, first it's entrapment, and second, I ain't sayin' jack shit, anyhow. Now if you'll excuse me."

He was about to climb out of the booth, but the pouty waitress was back with his second beer, which she set in front of him. She looked at me, as if to say, *Is this still on your tab?* And I nodded at her and she hipped off.

"Stay another beer's worth, Myron," I said pleasantly. "I just have a few questions, and they're not about your well-known sticky fingers."

He let a bunch of air out. Frowned. But he stayed.

Then he said, "Tuesday through Friday, I'm the only guy workin' that whole damn building. If things would start goin' missing, who do you *think* they'd look at?"

"Not the weekend guy. They'd check up on you, *really* check up this time, and somebody like Pat Chambers would tell them how you retired under pressure because of suspicion you're a damn thief, and the fuzz wouldn't bother with a wire. They'd just pull you in and grill you like one of the damn burgers in this joint.

They're a little small, the burgers, don't you think? Fries are pretty good, though."

He was confused now. The eyes were starting to look actually stupid. It occurred to me that maybe he had just the smarts to steal pocket money off a dead man and share stolen property with some fence. But blackmail a United States senator? I was starting to doubt it.

I cut to the chase. "I'm working for Senator Winters."

He looked genuinely surprised, even confused. "So?"

"So you tell me."

His shrug overdid it. "I run into the senator a couple of times. He has an office on the nineteenth floor... did he send you? I don't even really know him. If he says I took something, he's lying. He's usually gone by the time I come on."

"Is he?"

The ex-cop straightened. He hadn't touched the fresh beer yet. Then he managed, "I don't follow you."

"I understand Senator Winters works nights, now and then."

"Uh, sure... that's why I run into him a few times."

"Is it?"

"Is it... what?"

"Why you ran into him. Ever run into his secretary?"

His mouth dropped open. The stupidity was really outdistancing the smarts now. With his mouth open like that, he decided to fill it with beer, probably because he didn't know what to say.

"She's a looker," I reminded him. "Name's Lisa Long."

He swallowed some beer. Nodded. "I met *her* a couple times, too. Didn't know her name. She seems nice."

"Nice piece of tail, you mean? You have an eye for the ladies, don't you, Myron? Cost you a marriage, I understand. And a bunch of alimony, too, I bet."

He reddened. "What does Cindy have to do with this?"

"Who's Cindy?"

"My wife! Ex-wife..."

I chuckled. "Nothing. I don't know Cindy. I was just rattling your cage a little. Myron, what do you know about Lisa Long and the senator?"

A lesser shrug. "They work together."

"Take another run at that."

He smiled like a naughty boy with a secret. Then he blurted it: "He bangs her pretty regular. Whenever he's in town, he bangs that babe."

"Now we're getting somewhere."

He gulped the rest of the beer down, looked at the bartender again. Well, one thing was for sure—all these beers were going on the senator's expense account.

Leaning in, like we were suddenly buddies, the ex-cop said, "She's not the *only* one."

"She isn't?"

"No! I started at the Flatiron before that Lisa What's-It ever worked for that Winters clown. He had another secretary before that, he's banging. And sometimes he had other babes in there. I'm telling you, that son of a bitch gets more tail than Sinatra!"

Who was singing "New York, New York" again. I swear. That playing over and over on the jukebox was probably why the help here was so surly.

Very quietly, I said, "What if I told you somebody was blackmailing the senator?"

He laughed. Not the reaction of a blackmailer caught at it, I have to say.

He said, "I ain't surprised. Guy like that—he's got a babe for a wife, too, you know. She's in the *News* all the time, with her tits hangin' out. That redhead, what's her name?"

"Nicole Vankemp."

"Right! How many babes does one asshole need?"

I could have asked him the same question, but instead I said, "Have you met her, the senator's wife?"

"No."

"Let me rephrase that—have you seen her? Has she ever been around the office?"

He shook his head. "Not on my shift. But why would she? Her, he can bang at home."

Good point. Maybe Henry had been a hell of a detective, in his day.

"Myron, do you have a tape of the senator enjoying some after-hours nookie with his secretary?"

He frowned. "What, a video or something?"

"Or anything. An audio cassette, say."

He shrugged one shoulder. "Hell, I still got an *eight-track* in my car."

So he was either smarter or dumber than I'd thought.

"What if I told you," I said, "that an operative of mine is searching your house in the Bronx for that tape, even as we sit here enjoying a beer and each other's manly company?"

He grunted a laugh. "I'd say, I hope he's good with pit bulls, your operative, because *my* pit bull has the run of the place when I'm gone." Then he frowned. "Hey, if your guy puts a slug in Clarence, I'll kick his ass from here to Sunday. That pooch cost me two hundred bucks! He's got papers!"

I didn't think he meant he put papers down for the animal.

I raised a hand. "That was a bluff, my friend. But I'll tell you what isn't a bluff: if you're behind this blackmail scheme, I will tell Captain Chambers all about it, which I haven't yet. And when you get out of stir, we'll see what kind of security job you can land."

"Hey! You best back the hell off!"

"No, thanks. Now. My client prefers to keep this quiet. In fact, we could negotiate a generous payment, if you hand over the tape and any copies. But if we make such an agreement, and you break it, Myron—it won't be your pit bull that takes a slug."

The former cop/current security guard could have reacted any number of ways. He was younger than me and tough in his way, although he surely knew of my reputation. Still, he might have laughed me off and made a genuine denial, or half dozen other things.

But what he said was, "Hell, man—I wish I *had* that tape. Wish I'd thought of recording that horny politico and one of his honeys. I'd sell you that thing and you'd never hear from me again. I'd get out of this damn city and live high on the hog, somewhere." He shook his head. "But that's what I get for playing it straight, huh?"

He thanked me for the beers, with no sarcasm at all, and downed the last one before heading out to his job at the Flatiron Building.

CHAPTER FIVE

No question about it—the combination of preening oddballs and wide-eyed tourists in Greenwich Village always gives me a pain.

But some of the best entertainment in town could be seen and heard there, from the Village Vanguard and the Blue Note to the Bitter End and Bottom Line. And the piano bars on Grove Street were where you might find Velda and me, when the mood struck us.

Not that such venues as Marie's Crisis, The Five Oaks and Rose's Turn—all on the same tree-lined street a few doors from each other—didn't have their shortcomings. They crouched in low-slung basements foggy with cigarette smoke, their sound systems like carnival booth loudspeakers, the bathrooms a horror show, though the strength of their cocktails could not be denied.

Rose's Turn perched in space vacated by the Duplex, when it moved to Christopher Street. Downstairs, the former owners had left behind the black baby grand, the record-shop-poster-adorned brick walls, and the little black candle-lit tables, each crowded by four battered black chairs. Also a reputation as an intimate piano bar with character. An example of the latter was the time a guy at the bar unzipped and suddenly relieved himself with the velocity of a racehorse, the singer at the mike lifting her left foot to avoid the stream as she shifted from "Just One of Those Things" to "Cry Me a River."

This was not the first time Velda and I had gone through the double doors under the black awning with ROSE'S TURN in white. Sometimes we'd climb the dark stairs to the second-floor cabaret whose stage had been graced by the likes of Woody Allen, Richard Pryor, and Joan Rivers, or (as was the case tonight) we'd take the seven steps down to the piano bar, where lesser-known but no less talented performers shared the microphone with singing wait staff and well-oiled civilians.

This was, however, the first time we had gone to Rose's on business. We had not dressed for a night on the town, and were still in what we'd worn to the office today. Right now we were comparing notes on our respective investigative endeavors. I started with my visit to Pat's office and the sharing beers with ex-cop/current security guard Myron Henry. Then, stopping occasionally to sip at her glass of white wine, Velda told me about her afternoon and early evening, which had been spent here in the Village.

I found Helen Wayne (Velda said) *at the register in the Paper Book Gallery—over on Sullivan and West Third? Did you know they still have Beat-style poetry readings there? Good-looking young woman. Casually dressed, oversized sweater, jeans, short brown hair, permed like in her photo. Not much make-up. Not surprising she turned out to still be a nice girl from the Midwest.*

I bought a copy of The Beauty Myth *and she smiled and said 'Fine choice"—she'd read it and liked it herself. That's when I told her I was an investigator working with the* Daily News—*as you suggested, Mike—and that her name had turned up in the background inquiry on a story about Senator Winters. She seemed more intrigued than alarmed, and agreed to have a coffee with me on her break, in twenty minutes.*

So we sat in a coffee shop across the way and I at first said that we had learned she and Senator Winters had an affair. I told her the reporter had no intention of using her name, but we wanted to hear her side of things. She didn't say anything for a long while, and I was just starting to think she was going to get up and leave me hanging. But then she said, "What do you want to know?"

Rather than ask questions, I suggested she share her story with me. She nodded and said that was fine with her. She would appreciate confidentiality, but she was willing to talk to me. She was a very articulate young woman, Mike, and seemed fairly sophisticated for her age... I think that came not from her Ohio upbringing but her time already spent here in New York.

Anyway, she spoke highly of the senator. She believed in him, in the causes he espoused, and admired him for what he was trying to do for minorities and the poor and the rights of women.

"What a wonderful orator he is," she told me. "Did you know he writes all his own speeches?"

Yes, you're right, Mike—she does sound like she's still in love with him. Or at least enamored or whatever. But she feels quite the opposite about Mrs. Winters.

"That woman is a monster," she told me. "She has been cheating on the senator for years and years. She plays at being for the same kind of causes as Jamie, but it's all for show. For how she'll look in the media and to her rich friends."

She said that Winters had broken off the relationship, and this is exactly what she said, Mike—"gently and respectfully." He told Helen Wayne he loved her but he couldn't risk what he hoped to accomplish in politics if he "strayed from the straight and narrow." Right! Gag me with a spoon, as the younger generation says.

Helen says the senator told her that he was reconciling with his wife, and that Nicole had broken off her latest affair and intended to behave herself "henceforth." Did Helen believe Mrs. Winters would do that? Actually, yes. Why? Oh, for her own selfish reasons—to be the famous wife of a famous man, maybe even a president.

"Can you imagine her as First Lady?" she asked me.

Funny how she could feel such contempt for the woman but only admiration for the man, when the couple's goals appeared so similar.

I then told her she didn't need to worry about her name getting in the papers. That I wasn't really working with a journalist, but for the senator himself. Because someone was trying to blackmail him.

Her first reaction to that was concern for Winters. That it was terrible, unfair and so on. It took her a while to think of herself, and to realize that she might be the cause of the blackmail!

Why would she assume that? Well, in the sense that... Mike, remember, she claims no knowledge of the senator's other affairs. As far as she knows, she's the only woman. Or I should say... the only other *woman.*

No, of course I didn't say anything about the audio recording. If I'd gone that way, it would have been easy to at least imply that it was her on the tape. But I didn't. I just warned her that somebody had targeted the senator for blackmail, presumably for money but possibly to damage him politically. And gave her our card so that if anyone approached her, or anything unusual or unexpected relating to her time as the senator's secretary should come up, she could get in touch. Should *get in touch.*

"It never occurred to her," I said, "that she might be a suspect?"

Velda shook her head, raven arcs swinging. "No. I did ask her if she was seeing anyone right now, and she said no."

"You believe her?"

"I do." Her eyebrows chased her hairline. "If she's lying, if she's dissembling? She's really wasting her time behind a bookstore counter—she has a real career in acting ahead of her."

I sipped my CC and ginger. We were at a table as far away from the little performing area as possible. At the baby grand, a skinny dark-haired guy in an open-collar white shirt and dark slacks, who was born well after any of the Gershwin tunes he was playing, was having a nice jazzy way with them.

"Okay," I said. "You saw the McGuire girl, too?"

"I did. In some ways very similar to Ms. Wayne, in others not at all."

Judy, and she told me to call her that (Velda went on), *works at the White Horse Tavern. No, the place hasn't changed at all since last we were there—are you kidding? Same portraits of Dylan Thomas on the walls, same plaque celebrating his last drink there. I can't confirm what you claimed to see in the men's room is still visible…*

Velda referred to the "Go home, Jack!" scrawled in a stall, referring to Jack Kerouac, who was well known for getting tossed out of the joint, the inebriated author of *On the Road* being told frequently to hit the road.

…but I think Judy really likes the literary vibe, all the stories about Faulkner and Fitzgerald and Steinbeck being regulars. I don't think it's an accident that the two former Winters side dishes are both working at such literate if low-paying jobs. Both taking college courses, remember. I have a

feeling the senator likes them good-looking and *smart. So do* you, *you say? That your idea of a compliment, Mike?*

Anyway, Judy took her break with me, too, but we stayed right there at the White Horse in a back booth. Both had iced tea. She's wearing her hair long, but minus the current big perm treatment, not blonde like in the picture we were given—a light brown now, her real color I'd say. So, I gave her the same routine, Daily News, *background for an in-depth piece on the senator, because of all the chatter about him maybe going after that Pennsylvania Avenue address. And so on.*

Physically, all of these young women are the same type. Curvy, more cute than beautiful, outgoing personalities. Not unlike Mrs. Winters, if she hadn't been born to money and prone to… excess? Judy had the same opinions as Helen about the senator and his good causes. Maybe even more so. Right, she was a campaign worker so that was to be expected.

Different how? Oh. Well, I don't think Judy ever had a thought that something serious was going on between her and the senator. It's pretty clear she thinks he felt something for her. He said he loved her, *that he was crazy about her and all. That he wanted to divorce his wife and marry her.*

But Judy says she knew it was just talk. Oh, maybe he believed it, you know… at the moment? But on reflection, she knew he was a powerful man with a rich, famous wife, and she was just a young campaign worker, who… and these are her words… "got his juices going."

Well, "star fucker" is a little harsh, Mike… but maybe not inaccurate. He's famous, Judy is young, a kid from upstate getting to travel in rarefied circles. You've never heard "travel" used as a euphemism before, Mike? You need to expand your horizons.

Yes, yes, I shifted to the blackmail topic, told her the News *bit was phony and that I was working for the senator. The only thing… well, maybe a little* off *about it... is she asked me if* I *was with him now. And "with" clearly was a euphemism. I told her no, that I was a private detective working with another, very famous private detective, Mike Hammer himself... no, she never heard of you.*

"So fleeting, fame," I said, and sipped the drink, which was way more CC than ginger. They didn't scrimp at Rose's Turn, that was for sure. "So what's your take on the McGuire woman?"

Velda's dark eyes were steady. "She immediately wanted to know if the senator was being blackmailed specifically over *their* affair. Unlike Helen Wayne, Judith McGuire has no illusions that Senator Winters had never had an affair before... or since, for that matter."

"No kidding?"

"Oh yeah. She said he was the type. She knew that out of the gate. She said the way he looked at her at the job interview told her that if she took the job, she'd be taking on more than one kind of dictation."

I allowed myself a little smile at that. "She have a current boyfriend?"

"No."

"Believe her?"

"Maybe. We might want to put an operative on her tail."

"Since she never heard of me, I could put myself on her tail."

"I bet you could. So let's use somebody from the outside. She's never heard of you, remember? Let's keep it that way."

I grinned at her and she tried not to smile.

The skinny pianist in the white shirt got up and went to a standing microphone in front of the framed REMEMBER THE PIANO

PLAYER request for tips. He said, "Ladies and gentlemen, Rose's Turn presents its favorite songbird, Miss Nora Kent!"

A curvy little platinum blonde materialized from somewhere. She wore a clingy, old-fashioned glittery black gown with a low neckline that she did justice to, her hair a big frizzy nest on loan from Bernadette Peters. I had a feeling her get-up and song choice were supposed to be campy, so wrong for today it was tomorrow, but all I could think about was the yesterday of Peggy Lee and Julie London. Her heart-shaped face was home to a generous mouth painted so red it made your eyes water, and her silver-shadowed eyes weren't any bigger or bluer than the Gulf of Mexico.

She started with "Somebody Loves Me," in a breathy but right-on-pitch alto that made the room seem even smokier than it already was. The piano player, back at his post, stayed right with her, adding percussion to his already deft noodling. This was exactly what you wanted out of a piano bar. And I would remember him with a tip.

She sang maybe a dozen standards—"It Had to Be You," "Black Coffee," a few peppier things, "Fly Me to the Moon," "If You Ask Me, I Could Write a Book," winding up with "I'll Be Seeing You." That one could have made a weaker World War Two veteran tear up some. If I did, it was surely all that smoke.

Velda and I chatted for a while, mostly about how good Nora Kent was, both of us really impressed. Velda had arranged with the young woman to talk to us after her set. We were waiting for the girl when a waitress came over in a green-and-black plaid shirt and jeans. Her hair was pixie short and as black as Velda's and she wore no make-up on her cute, young face.

Only she wasn't a waitress.

"Miss Sterling?" she said to Velda. Then to me: "Mr. Hammer?"

This was Nora Kent, minus the clingy dress, Hollywood make-up and giant frizzy wig.

I half-stood, gestured to the chair between Velda and me. She sat. As big as her presence at the mike had been, she was a little thing here.

"Thanks for agreeing to talk to us," Velda said.

"You're welcome," she said, her speaking voice higher than her singing one. She was a kid, really. Probably not twenty-five yet. In addition to being a hound, our client, the senator, is a consistent cradle robber.

She went on: "What sort of background are you looking for about Senator Winters?"

Velda hesitated, but I stepped up. "That was just a dodge, Nora. Is it all right if I call you that? And we'll make it Mike and Velda. This is a friendly get-together."

She narrowed her aqua eyes and looked from me to Velda and back. "Okay, Mike. Velda. But what do you mean, exactly? A 'dodge'?"

Velda said, "We frankly wanted to ascertain your attitude toward the senator. Whether it was positive or negative or… or what exactly."

"We know about the affair," I said quietly.

The pianist was playing tunes from *Gypsy*, now. That made sense, what with the place named after a song from that show. Right now it was "Small World."

"So," Nora said warily, but not getting up to go as she might have, "this *isn't* for an article. I won't be quoted or anything."

Velda said, "No. We just need to talk to you."

"Then what is this about—really?"

I said, "The senator is being blackmailed."

Her eyes widened, just briefly. But she was calm as she said, "About his women?"

I traded glances with Velda. "You're aware that he's had multiple affairs?"

She fingered a pack of cigarettes, Virginia Slims, in her plaid shirt's breast pocket. She got out a smoke, lit it off the table's central candle. She nodded as she got the cig going.

She raised one of the dark eyebrows that with the silver shadow were all that remained of her make-up at the mike. "I knew he was... what's the old-fashioned word? A rounder. I wondered if he might not get in trouble over that, one of these days."

"Our understanding," Velda said, "is that the senator was a one-woman man, where his affairs are considered."

"One-woman-at-a-time man," I further clarified.

She nodded. "He told sad stories of marital discord. How his wife cheated on him, from the beginning. How they hadn't made love in years." Her smile was as big as it was ironic. "He loved *me*, did you know that? Wanted to *marry* me."

I said, "You didn't believe any of it."

"Not for a heartbeat," she said, and exhaled smoke, not seeming young at all now. "Oh, he was genuinely taken with me. He was one of those men who is in love with being in love. But eventually he tires."

Velda asked, "Did he tire of you?"

She smiled. The way she held her cigarette in an outwardly angled hand was as yesterday as her singing style. "Not quite yet, he hadn't. But I sensed it."

I asked, "What were the signs?"

"The way he looked at waitresses. The way he looked at women passing in the street. He likes women. And not just sexually. He likes brains. He likes talent. Tell me, that secretary—Helen something? She quit right after Jamie and I started up. *They* were a thing, weren't they?"

Velda and I both nodded.

She smiled and this time the smoke came out her nostrils, dragon-style. She looked seventeen. She looked a hundred and seventeen.

"He was here at the Turn with some friends of his," she said. "Probably business stuff. Potential campaign donors, maybe. Powerful men of industry. Possibly other political types in town for something or other. Anyway, he came here one night with some men and saw me, and then did the same a few nights later, minus any male company. He sent a note back to me, asked me to join him."

Velda said, "How direct was he?"

A shrug. "Oh, he was subtle enough. That first night all he talked about was my singing and how much he liked the American Songbook stuff—Gershwin, Cole Porter, Johnny Mercer. Took several weeks for us to get into bed."

Velda and I exchanged glances again.

"Look, he's a handsome man," she said, not defensive, just explaining. "Very smooth. Nice to be around. *Fun* to be around.

And a hell of a lover. Thoughtful, too. Strictly safe sex, which in this day and age is about as thoughtful as it gets."

I said, "I'm going to take a wild swing and say you weren't in love with him."

"Mike," she said, with half a smile, "I haven't been in love since the high-school quarterback knocked me up and I had to pay for getting rid of it out of my college savings."

She must have made it to Julliard on a scholarship.

"So," I said, with a shrug, "you and the senator—that was just for kicks?"

"For kicks and for… well, he's obviously well-connected. Used to be a top publicist, you know. I thought Jamie might whisper in the ear of one of his Broadway benefactors. I do whispery stuff here, getting the girls wet and the guys hard. But I can be heard in the back row, if I need to."

I said, "So it was all about his show business connections."

She shrugged a single shoulder. "To some degree. But I *did* like him. And he was generous. Money. Gifts." She opened her eyes wide and half-smirked. "How much do you think I make *here*?"

Velda said, "You're very good. I would imagine you do all right."

"Tips and a stipend. You want to know part of what the appeal was with the senator? Free meals. He took me to some very nice, very expensive, very out-of-the-way places. There were trips, too. Cancun. The Bahamas." She shrugged, tamped her cigarette ash in a glass ROSE'S TURN tray. "Fun while it lasted."

"Are you blackmailing him?" I asked. "Maybe you and your latest boyfriend?"

She laughed. "Do I look desperate? And the guys I run into here, both on staff and in the audience, are mostly gay." She flashed me an impish smile. "All the *real* macho men, Mike, are taken."

I grunted a laugh. "I'm old enough to be your father, honey."

"You're older than my father. But also richer. I know who you are, Mr. Hammer. You're famous in this town."

At least some of the young babes had heard of me.

"If you *are* blackmailing the senator," I said, "tell me right now. And we'll settle up."

"Are you wearing a wire?"

"No. Search me if you like."

Her eyes were half-lidded. "You wish. I'm a lot of things, Mr. Hammer, Ms. Sterling... but I am *not* a blackmailer. And I doubt this is about money, anyway, at least not directly so. This is probably the usual dirty politics. Even today, a guy on his way to the White House can be taken down by sexual indiscretions. He should be satisfied with being senator and having that rich, sexy wife of his. Is there anything else?"

I said, "Blackmail can lead to some very dark places, Ms. Kent. If you are approached by someone who wants to involve you in this scheme, I'd advise you to get in touch."

I handed her a card and she took it. Studied it like a check that might have been added up wrong.

I went on: "If anything out of the ordinary occurs, anything disturbing, anything in particular related to the senator and/or your time with him... let us know. I like your way with a song. I wouldn't care to see you behind bars or get hurt."

Her voice small, suddenly, she said, "That's not a threat, is it?"

I raised a palm. "Not at all. It's an offer of help, if you need it.

But if you're part of this blackmailer's business, it won't be help you get from me. That's a promise, not a threat."

She thought about that. Nodded. Tucked the card in the breast pocket behind the pack of Virginia Slims. Put the current cigarette out in the glass tray and said, "Thanks for the compliment. About my singing." She nodded to Velda, said, "Ms. Sterling," then threaded off through the tables.

"Well?" Velda asked.

I was watching the young woman go. "She's capable of being on the wrong side of this."

"I agree. But every one of these three women is smart enough to play us, *and* the senator."

"Four women," I said, holding up that many fingers. "Lisa Long is smart, too."

Velda shook her head. "No. The current secretary's a victim. I think you were on the right track with that intercom set-up. *That's* where the sex tape came from. If not from the security guy, then the cleaning woman."

"One more woman to talk to," I said sourly. "It'll wait till tomorrow."

Velda finished her wine, leaned back, folded her arms, and gave me a smug smile. "You're just awash in babes on this job, aren't you, Mr. Hammer? Just one young doll after another. Sounds like your dream case to me."

I held up a surrendering palm. "No, it's a nightmare. They're all too young and I'm too damn old."

"Not too old for me, Mike." She wiggled the hand with the engagement rock on it. "Maybe it's time to settle down."

I shrugged. "Let's see what the cleaning lady looks like first."

She grinned and slapped me on the arm.

Then we paid the check and got the hell out of there. I might have stayed to listen to another of Nora Kent's sets, but I'd heard enough of her singing already.

CHAPTER SIX

The Fifth Avenue of the Flatiron Building was one thing—the Fifth Avenue across the river in Brooklyn was something else again. This grim stretch—wide-open drug deals, bodega cashiers in Plexiglas cages and SMACK KILLS graffiti, Salvation Army storefronts operating like frontier forts—cut through the Park Slope neighborhood like a junkie's ravaged, ragged arm.

Park Slope was in the midst of a nervous breakdown, with gentrification under way even as a crack house popped up near venerable Prospect Park, baseball on offer but coke 8-balls too, a nice area where shootings and muggings were becoming commonplace. The neighborhood was "in transition," the Realtors would say. This was the kind of area, after all, where educated middle-class couples lived alongside working-class Irish, Italian, and Puerto Rican immigrants in an area once known as the Borough of Churches.

Erin Dunn's Park Slope address on Seventh Avenue was an apartment in a somewhat renovated brownstone, a once-proud four-story that was a ripe prospect for either gentrification or arson, but right now was just another shabby structure that took in boarders.

It was a quarter to noon. I'd figured to allow the cleaning lady to get in a few hours of sleep before dropping by on her. Getting her phone number and calling her up first would be courteous, but a bad idea in this situation.

The day was cold and crisp and overcast again, so the hat and trenchcoat were required. Whether the .45 was or not, who could say? But I always packed heat on criminal matters. I'd considered taking the subway, but I hadn't had the heap out of the parking garage for maybe a month and figured to take my nondescript black Ford with its souped-up motor out for a ride. Shake the rust off. The drive in steady but unclogged traffic gave me a chance to think.

While I wasn't ruling Myron Henry out, the ex-cop didn't seem like a good bet for the blackmail route. And none of the four women that either Velda or I or both of us had talked to seemed likely accomplices in an extortion scheme, either. Still, you never knew. And how would a working-class woman like Erin Dunn get caught up in a blackmail scheme involving a United States senator?

Plenty of options here, just no good ones.

Parking on the street was no problem. But it took repeated knocking to get me a haggard, rheumy-eyed woman in her late seventies with smudged scarlet lipstick and white hair whose perm was a dim memory. Her blue-and-green floral housedress was faded and torn, her thick stockings saggy, her shoes brown and clunky.

"Not buying," she rasped through the cracked door.

"Not selling," I said, and showed her the P.I. badge in the leather fold. That almost always works. It did now.

"You got the wrong house, officer," she said, chin going up proudly. "We're respectable here. I don't take in druggies and Mr. Davis is my only alkie, and he come straight from rehab."

She started to close the door on me. That's what a detective's gum-sole shoe is for.

I shouldered in with a smile.

"Good to hear," I said. "But I'm not looking for a drug addict or an alcoholic that I know of. Unless one of those categories applies to Erin Dunn."

The entryway announced corned beef and cabbage from a kitchen visible down the hall, bordered by an open stairway. To my left I saw a mahogany-edged parlor where furnishings with faded upholstery were arranged on worn oriental rugs on oak parquet floors. A struggle had been going on for years here, between respectability and atrophy. Respectability was losing.

"Miss Dunn is no druggie or alkie or nothin'. A good girl, as far as it goes."

"Is she in?"

The crone nodded. "Works nights in the city."

"Yes, she's a cleaning woman at the Flatiron Building. Is she married?"

"No. But she lives with a dago fella. People *used* to have morals."

"Why, is Erin an immoral type, do you think?"

She shook her head. "No more or less than anybody these days, I suppose. She works a respectable job, anyway. Her man just tends bar over at Snooky's up the street."

I took a little offense. "Bartender's a respectable job. My old man was a bartender."

"Be that as it may, Snooky's ain't no respectable joint, that's for ding dang sure. You're not Brooklyn PD, are ya?"

"No. My beat's in Manhattan." Not claiming to represent the police, you'll note. And I *was* an officer of the court, remember. "What's the, uh, dago's name?"

"Tony Something. They're *all* Tony Somethings, ain't they?"

"Well, I've known a Mario or two. Is Tony up there?"

She shrugged. "Ain't my day to look after him. But the Dunn girl's up and around. Come down for the mail. Are you going up there?"

"Her room's upstairs?"

She nodded. "Top right. 2A. Tell her if she wants lunch, I ain't serving past 1:30."

So it was a rooming house, not apartments.

"You want some lunch, officer?"

"That's nice of you, ma'am, but—"

"Cost a buck. Bargain at twice the price. You know what corned beef is a pound these days?"

I admitted I didn't, and headed up the stairs. She trundled back toward the kitchen. She'd have some non-druggies and ex-alkies to serve soon.

The stairs had remnants of carpeting where you stepped, but that didn't stop the creaking. A general musty odor danced with the corned beef and cabbage. I would have blackmailed somebody gladly, to get out of that place.

I knocked at 2A.

The face that appeared was a narrow, lightly freckled oval offset by apple cheeks. Her eyes were sky blue but bore a red filigree—either she'd been crying or she was just plain tired. Her hair was red, but not the Nicole Winters variety—this shade didn't come from a beauty shop but strictly from genes. She wore it short and curly. No perm, either. No make-up at all, not that she needed it.

"Yes?" she said, cracking the door suspiciously, much as her landlady had. A pleasant enough voice but no Irish lilt, that was for sure.

"Need a word, Ms. Dunn," I said, and flashed the badge.

It worked on her, too.

The door opened and I stepped in and she closed it behind me, looking at me warily.

Then she led me into a very neat room—her cleaning skills on display here, as well—of furnishings that were either secondhand or had haphazardly assembled themselves over the decades in this house, the kind of things you relegated to a guest room when you really didn't like having guests. Chairs from the 1950s joined tables from the '30s, and an overstuffed sofa from the '40s with springs trying to escape had blond end tables with an early '60s atomic style.

Erin Dunn was something else again.

She wore a green satin robe—her red hair went well with emerald, just as Nicole's had—sashed at the waist. The sleek fabric clung enough to show off a busty figure with nice gams showing at the knee. Her feet were bare. This was another small, curvy female, like the others in this case, with Nicole and of course Velda the only leggy exceptions.

"Won't you sit down, officer?" she asked, gesturing to a well-worn easy chair positioned across from the sofa, where she settled herself. She crossed her legs, revealing some creamy inner thigh.

She wasn't showing off, but then she didn't have to.

Before I sat, I draped my trenchcoat over the back of the chair and tossed my hat on the coffee table between us. Maybe it was that term—"cleaning lady"—that had made me expect something dowdy, or a woman heavy-set, or anything but another foxy addition to the chorus line this case was turning into.

But Erin Dunn was a beauty, all right. Maybe not a raving one, but certainly a little doll who might well have earned the attentions of a certain United States senator. Had my client withheld the identity of one of his conquests? It would hardly be the first time a client lied to me.

She sat forward, hands clasped, her eyes wide now. "Uh, officer, I don't have any coffee going, but I can get us some downstairs, if you like."

"No, that's fine. Thank you, though. Get yourself a cup, if you want. This may take a while."

She shook her head, the tight red curls hardly moving. She reached for a pack of cigarettes, Kools, on the nearby end table and lighted up from a book of matches. She waved out the flame, got the smoke going, and only then said, "You don't mind, do you?"

"No," I said, and smiled a little. "I'm an ex-smoker and relish any secondhand smoke that comes along."

She smiled a little, too. "So. What's this about?"

"I have a few questions about your job at the Flatiron Building."

Her pause was brief, but it nonetheless registered on me.

She said, "Go right ahead. I have nothing to hide."

It's been my experience that the only people who say they have nothing to hide usually have something to hide. But not always.

I said, "How long have you worked at the Flatiron?"

Her smile was quick and gone. "Well, I should straighten you out on that."

"Please do."

She gestured with the Kool in hand. "I don't actually work for the Flatiron. Not itself. I work for a cleaning service that contracts with the building. There are five of us girls. One strictly cleans the men's and ladies' rooms. I clean the upper floors—seventeen up. It's a lot of work in a short period of time."

"An eight-hour 'day'?"

She nodded, drew in smoke, let it out. "Eight-hour shift, yes."

"That includes the nineteenth floor."

"Of course."

"So Senator Winters' office is on your list."

"It is. He's not there all the time, only certain days, certain times of the year. So that's one of the easy ones. I can skip it, frequently. Why? Is there a concern about the senator's office?"

"Yes. Something was taken."

Her eyes widened. But there was something artificial about her reaction. "Really? That surprises me."

"Why is that?"

She shrugged. "Well, nothing terribly valuable's in that particular office. Some others have paintings and sculptures that I would imagine are worth money. I'm not an expert on such things. Oh! The computer and so on—was *that* what was taken?"

"No."

"Then maybe you should tell me what was."

I sat back, sighed big, as if the day had already worn me out.

"You know, I think I *will* have that coffee."

She got up quickly, her expression pleasant, lips pursed in a smile. "Certainly. Sugar? Cream?"

"Both, please."

She put her cigarette out in a tray, said, "I won't be long," and went out.

I could hear her padding down the creaky stairs.

I got up and poked around, but something told me she'd expected that. As if she wanted to prove to me she hadn't taken anything from the senator's office. Whether she was specifically thinking of a cassette tape, I had no idea.

In this outer room, a little writing desk and some odd pieces with drawers all proved unhelpful. Adjacent was a cubbyhole kitchenette. The only other room was the bedroom, where the neat little female had already made the bed, and where nothing in the dresser or nightstand drawers gave up anything of note. I didn't check the closet, other than to just peek in quickly, before going back out and resuming my chair.

No bathroom in the place. This was a rooming house with shared facilities. Nothing fancy here, and what made it barely livable was the fastidiousness of a woman who made her living cleaning for others, and brought that bent home.

She came in with a little tray and cups of coffee for both of us. My coffee had already been sugared and creamed. She was having hers black. Resuming her seat, she placed the coffee cup on its saucer on the atomic end table and sat close to that arm of the sofa. Crossed her legs again. Very pretty legs, but still she wasn't showing off. Just getting comfortable, and she seemed at ease, though I had a hunch she was neither of those things.

So I pretended to just be making conversation, between sips of the coffee. If that old gal downstairs had made this stuff, she had at least one talent.

"Your landlady's quite a character," I said.

"She is at that," Erin said, laughing a little. "You should hear her talk about her clientele in 'better days.' It was all respectable bachelors and older women who had known finer times. She claims she served them tea on silver trays."

I smiled. "I'm happy with just the coffee. She's a talky one. Mentioned to me that you live with someone who's not just a roommate, I take it."

Her eyebrows went up and she made herself keep smiling. "Tony? Tony Licata, yes, we're, uh… engaged."

I gave her another smile. "Trial run never hurt anybody. Of course, if you ever have kids, you'll need bigger, better digs than this."

She nodded. Sighed. "True enough. This is a terrible place, officer. Most of the other boarders are old people, *really* old people—men and women on government assistance." She shivered. "Would *you* like to share a bathroom with the likes of them? Poor souls, but…" She shivered again. "No, not a place to have kids… we'd have to live better than *this*."

"Park Slope's improving, they say."

The big blue eyes widened. "Not fast enough! Any nights I'm not working, I almost always hear car windows getting shattered, by a baseball bat or whatever. Kids can't walk home from school without a parent playing escort. Do you know how many times I've been held up at gunpoint on my way home from the subway station?"

"Is that why you did it?"

"Did what?"

"Recorded the senator and his secretary going at it in the next room."

She swallowed. Her face turned whiter than a blister. She said, "I don't know what the hell you're talking about.... Let me see that badge again. Let me see your I.D.!"

I got out the leather fold and reached it out to her across the coffee table. She snatched it from me.

"Michael Hammer," she read. "I know that name. Private investigations!... Did I read about you in the paper? Are you who they wrote that story about?"

I shrugged. "I've had a lot of stories written about me. Maybe you're thinking of the nostalgia piece in the *Post* last year. 'Remember that trigger-happy private eye? He's still around!'"

She stood. She was shaking. Really trembling.

"You should leave," she said. "Right now."

I patted the air with my palms. "I'll leave. But hear me out, first."

"Why should I?"

"Because otherwise you might go to jail. At the very least you'll lose your job and never be employable again in your trade. And you are a lovely young woman obviously adept at cleaning up for others. You should try cleaning up for yourself... while you still can."

She narrowed her eyes about halfway through that, really thinking, thinking. She sat, her knees together now. Her hands on her thighs.

"First," I said, "I need you to be straight with me about

something, and remember—I can check it, easy enough. You see, the senator and his wife are my clients. The senator, as you know, is being blackmailed."

"Not by me!"

"By Tony, then."

Her chin quivered. "Not... not exactly. I don't think I should say anything else. I think you should go."

"Not just yet. We have a few questions to get through, first. Let's start with, have you ever been involved with the senator? I can get the truth out of him, if you don't want to give it to me."

Her eyes were very wide now. "Involved... you mean *involved*? No! I've only *spoken* to him a few times. He doesn't know I exist."

"Oh, he does now. So tell me if I'm mistaken about any of this. The senator and Ms. Long were playing hide the salami in his inner office and either the intercom had been left on, or you knew how to utilize it to record their fun and games. You replaced the cassette with a blank one from one of the secretary's desk drawers and tucked the little audio love-fest in your pocket. But not, you say, for blackmail reasons?"

She was looking at her lap, where her hands were folded now. She was shaking her head. "You'll never believe me."

"Take a swing."

"I did it as a joke. A... a lark."

"Explain."

Her smile was a wrinkled thing. "Tony, he's a... he's a real character. He likes a good laugh. He's... really into sex stuff." She shook her head and smiled. "Hey, we're into each other, okay? You got a problem with that?"

"None. Sounds very healthy to me."

She sighed. Very big. "Well, I thought Tony would get a kick out of the tape. A charge out of it. I thought he'd think it was a real riot, hearing a big shot like Senator Winters getting it on with his secretary. I thought... oh hell. I could see us listening to that and getting all hot and... I can't talk about this."

"So it was Tony who had the idea."

She nodded. "He listened to it and he didn't react like I figured. Instead, he... he just started to pace around. He said, think how if we could get some *real* money, we could move into a decent place and finally get married. We'd really have something to build on."

Blackmail. Something to build on.

"Anyway," she said, "I... I went along. But it wasn't about blackmailing the senator."

"It wasn't?"

"No! Tony said he knew just who to sell it to. Don't ask me who that is, because I don't know. I really don't. But Tony, he's a bartender, you know?"

"A noble profession."

"Yeah, well, he's good at it, and he's had some really good jobs—it's not just joints like Snooky's and Moody's. Worked some of the big hotels, when they needed additional help for parties or whatever. Some of those parties have important people at them. Businessmen. What do you call it, captains of industry? And big shot politicians."

"Like Senator Winters."

"Yeah, but *not* Senator Winters, too. Other people in that area, that field. Listen, Mr. Hammer—that's really all I know."

I studied her. "Are you saying that Tony sold that tape already? Not to the senator, but to someone else?"

"Yes! And that someone else must be the blackmailer you're after!"

I sat forward. "Listen, Erin—I'm in a position to protect you on this. I can even protect Tony. He doesn't *deserve* it, but I can. All the senator wants is to stop this—to stop the blackmailer, and get that tape deep-sixed...."

Somebody worked a key in the door.

A big good-looking guy in a bomber jacket with a fur collar and jeans and motorcycle boots let himself in. His hair was dark and curly, his eyes were half-lidded, and his mouth had that Stallone looseness. Maybe twenty-five, he looked like he could bench-press a Buick.

Erin flew to her feet.

"Baby!" she said. "This is Mike Hammer! He's here to help us out of this mess."

He shrugged, stepped inside, but left the door standing open. His voice was a thick baritone, like Elvis if he had no sense of humor. "What mess?"

"Somebody's blackmailing Senator Winters with that tape," she said. "Mr. Hammer says if we're honest with him, he'll get us out of this thing."

He looked at me, dark eyes tight. "We wouldn't have to pay the money back?"

"If you sold that tape, and didn't keep any copies," I said, "you can swim in that money as far as I'm concerned. All we want is the name of who you sold it to."

He came slowly over to me. "You could keep the law off of us?"

"Very good chance of that."

His frown was confused, no threat in it at all. "That doesn't sound like 'yes'."

I held one palm up. "I can see a situation where, if the cops got onto this, you might have to testify. But you'd likely get immunity."

"And you'll pave the way for that?"

"I will."

He nodded, then extended his hand for me to shake and, as I extended mine and leaned toward him, he brought that hand quickly back and turned it into a fist and slammed it into the side of my face.

I didn't go down, didn't lose my balance, but my head swam— he was as big as me but much younger, and if he had kept at it, he might have got enough good ones in to put me down and out.

Instead, he used those few seconds while I was stunned to bolt for the open door. He was halfway down the stairs before I made my way after him, and a guy my age should not have done what I did.

But I did.

I threw myself at him, threw myself down those stairs and tackled him, taking his ass down. Then I rode the bastard like a sled down those steps, each one banging him in the head and face. We wound up in a pile on the little landing, with only a few stairs left to go, and I got up and stepped over him and dragged him down a few more of those stairs, face-first, hauled him like a bag of laundry and tossed him in the entry way.

The crone of a landlady in her torn, faded housedress was standing nearby now, screaming her head off. It sounded like an old-time siren, the kind you had to crank. Somehow I got the front door open and I dragged him some more, but by his fur collar now—going down those cement steps face-first might have killed him, and I wanted him alive.

I tossed him onto the sidewalk and, catching my breath, I'll be damned but if he didn't tackle me and knock me back onto the sidewalk. He got on top of me, flailing at me with hard fists though without much power behind them, after the ride he'd taken.

So I kneed him in the nuts and he crawled off of me and curled up in a fetal ball and yelled bloody murder and started crying. A bawling ball of flesh.

Up on the front stoop, the old lady was screaming and now, next to her, the pretty Irish lass in a green satin robe was screaming, too.

The only one not making noise was me.

I was waiting till things quieted down so I could ask this son of a bitch a question.

CHAPTER SEVEN

I was anything but a regular at 21, Midtown's notoriously high-priced, celebrity-teeming bar/restaurant on West 52nd between Fifth and Sixth Avenues. On the other side of that famous iron gate, past the uniformed doorman and through the double entryway overseen by a row of white lawn jockeys, you could get duck-fat-fried hamburgers that cost as much as the club's name and king-size drinks no stronger than a mule kicking you in the stomach.

I'd been to the onetime speakeasy maybe four times in a lot of New York years. Apparently I still had enough local fame clinging to me to get into the bar without being shown back out the door. Or maybe the ex-governor of the state of New York who had said to meet him here for a late lunch had put in a good word.

Former governor Harrison "Harry" Hughes had seemed as surprised by my call as I had been to hear his name uttered through the bloodied lips of Tony Licata.

"Are you accusing me of blackmail, Mike?" the deep voice, sandpapered by age, had asked over the phone. I'd been calling from a booth on Fifth Avenue in Brooklyn, and he'd answered the call himself, not a secretary.

"I don't know if I'm accusing you of anything, Governor," I said. "Maybe you're just a good citizen who learned of compromising material about a fellow Democrat, and paid the freight to get it off the market."

The pause may have seemed longer because of the three black young men who, in the midst of some kind of business transaction, were watching me suspiciously outside a nearby bar. People tell me I still look like a cop, even when I'm not flashing my P.I. badge to encourage that false assumption.

Finally, the deep voice on the phone said, "I would prefer to discuss this with you in person."

Phone calls could be recorded, after all.

"Fine," I said. "Name the time and place."

Lunch and supper hours, 21 would be packed, bar and upstairs alike, but at around three p.m., the front section with its curved sixty-foot bar was decidedly underpopulated, a few well-dressed wheeler-dealers doing business there standing up (no stools provided). Most of the tables with their red-and-white checkered cloths, including those at the vast curving red leather button-tufted banquette, were empty, too. A couple of couples and a few tourists, who'd tipped their way in, were about it.

Framed *New Yorker* cartoon originals spotted the walls in the richly masculine place with its dark walls and low lighting. The ceiling hung with toys—airplane and auto models, foot- and basket- and baseballs, mini-soda pop trucks and oil derricks and you name it, contributions from various executives of the firms the playthings represented. On display above and around the bar itself were flags, pistols, street signs, golden horseshoes and a hangman's noose.

The ex-governor sat at a table for two snugged by the bar, in the corner. He was waiting patiently, his right elbow on the table but not with his weight on it. The drink at his reach appeared, judging by its amber shade and orange peel, to be an Old-Fashioned.

I paused at the bar. The white-haired, white-jacketed, black-bow-tied bartender smiled faintly and said, "The usual, Mr. Hammer?"

I had last been here perhaps ten years ago.

"Please," I said, curious to see how good his memory was.

The governor half-stood and smiled—not a big smile, but a smile all right—and offered his hand for me to take and shake. The result was a firm clasp, not at all clammy. I hadn't expected it to be.

Harry Hughes was a few years older than me. I had won a battlefield commission up to lieutenant by the time I mustered out, thanks to my Bronze Star. The governor had a Bronze Star, too, and a Silver Star. He came out a colonel. I had perhaps an inch on him, but he was still a big, broad-shouldered man, his black hair streaked silver, his well-grooved square face dominated by sharp dark eyes and a shovel jaw. The suit was charcoal and likely Brooks Brothers, his tie gray and black and crisply knotted.

"Would you like lunch, Mike? My treat."

We had met only a few times over the years, never had any business together, or major problems either, for that matter. Still, it didn't feel wrong for him to call me by my first name.

"I could go for one of those twenty-one-buck burgers," I said. Lunch had eluded me so far today.

"My choice as well," he said, gesturing for me to sit, and we both did.

The guy was a politician, so I didn't put anything past him. But that the search for a blackmailer had ended here was a shock and even a disappointment. Hughes had been a damn good governor. He was a tax-cutter and a builder, a tricky damn combination. He took office with the city near bankrupt, and worked with business and labor to deal with the fiscal crisis NYC suffered in the mid-'70s, and did all this while working with a divided statehouse. Though a Democrat, his middle-of-the-road style recalled another governor, Nelson Rockefeller, New York's favorite moderate Republican.

Hughes, a Catholic, hadn't been active on the political scene since a scandal a few years ago, involving his wife having concealed a previous marriage, which had embarrassed him in the media. She'd died of cancer a few years ago. In the meantime, he'd published an autobiography and a book extolling "reaching across the partisan divide." Lately he had begun making the rounds of the Sunday morning political talk-fests as a Grand Old Man speaking from experience and not ambition.

A white-jacketed waiter brought my drink. I sipped it. Rye and ginger. I turned and nodded at the bartender and he nodded back. Meanwhile, Hughes ordered us two burgers, medium rare.

"Governor," I said, when we were alone again, "I'm almost as surprised that you wanted to meet in a public place as I am to find myself talking to you on this particular subject."

His smile was a rumpled thing, like folds in fabric. He had a tan that said Florida, or maybe tropical vacations were a part of his retirement.

He said, "I figured I was safer meeting in public with a

roughneck like Mike Hammer. A man my age doesn't like to get slapped around."

"Now, Governor…"

The dark eyes damn near twinkled. "Back when I was in office, your… exploits were often called to my attention."

"Don't tell me you believe everything you read in the papers."

One side of the smile dug a hole in his cheek. "Some of your doings in those days didn't make it into the papers. Some I never got straight answers on. That warehouse on the Hudson, where all those supposed Soviet agents and fellow travelers wound up very dead… something like one hundred of them… *that* caught my attention. A tommy gun, yet."

"That's not really accurate, Governor."

One eyebrow arched. "In what way?"

"It was an abandoned paint factory."

The other eyebrow joined it. The mouth was still smiling, but those dark eyes weren't. "Perhaps I was right to be cautious, Mike."

I smiled at him, probably in just as rumpled a way. "We're both a couple of old soldiers, Governor."

"Getting older all the time." He raised his glass. "Here's to absent friends. The ones we left behind. Mine in Europe, yours in the Pacific."

I raised my glass. "To absent friends."

We clinked the drinks. Sipped.

I said, "You have nothing to worry from me, Governor. I was a young buck back then. I've mellowed."

Only half a smile now. "After I received your call, Mike, I made several calls of my own. Seems a certain young Anthony Licata is in serious condition in Brooklyn Medical."

"See? Time was he'd be in intensive care."

He chuckled at that, but his eyes were still hard. "Let's start with an essential fact—I did *not* put this thing into motion. I did *not* seek out this cleaning staff person—the Dunn woman—to ensnare Jamie Winters by way of a secret recording of one of his hanky-panky sessions."

"What *did* happen, Governor?"

His shrug was slow. "Licata is a young man I met at a few gatherings at various hotels in town where he was a pick-up bartender. He was affable enough, not unintelligent—we were friendly in that limited way one does with such people."

I sipped rye and ginger again. Said, "You're saying he knew you just well enough to seek you out, when he came into possession of the sex tape."

He winced. "Let's just call it a recording and leave it at that. I find this whole thing distasteful. I hope you understand that."

"I might understand it better," I said, "if you had acquired the 'recording' for disposal, rather than to profit from it. How much do you want for the wretched thing, Governor?"

He wasn't looking at me now. He was staring at nothing, or perhaps into himself. I had a hunch he really did find this affair distasteful.

The waiter brought us both another drink.

When Hughes didn't answer my question, I said, "Aren't you retired from the political racket, Governor? Why the interest in Jamie Winters at all? It's not like you're a political rival at this point."

His reaction was another smile, but a very different one—small, sad, and even… embarrassed?

His sigh seemed endless. "Mike, I *am* an old soldier. Somewhat older than you. But I think I have one more battle left in me, at least. And I am arrogant enough to imagine that I can still do something good in government—in *national* government."

Now I got it.

I said, "You're considering your own presidential run."

He nodded slowly, his eyes back on mine. "Many a former governor has become president. Most recently Jimmy Carter, with admittedly mixed results, accomplished it. And now this young Arkansas character is making noises for next time—word is *his* morals aren't any better than Winters'."

Hughes had apparently been overheard chatting about a possible presidential try at one or more of the parties where Tony Licata was bartending. That was how Erin Dunn's muscle-bound boyfriend knew where to peddle the sex tape.

Hughes was saying, "A popular, multi-term governor from an important state, like myself—if I might be so bold—could make a most attractive candidate." He pulled in a deep breath, raised his eyebrows, let the breath out. "Since Evelyn's death, I gradually came to feel that perhaps I had one more bridge worth crossing."

"A last hurrah," I said.

"I admit I did not relish a primary where I'd be facing an attractive candidate—attractive in the sense of being young and handsome, that is—in Jamie Winters. But as a resident of this city and of this state, I have had ample opportunity to view the callow, amoral nature of that man, as is demonstrated by his reckless philandering... and then, of course, there's his reprehensible disco queen of a wife."

"Nicole Winters comes from money," I said, "and is clearly a spoiled brat. But she's also been active in social causes for years, particularly those that you Democrats seem to espouse." I shrugged. "You could argue that she's done a lot of good."

He batted that away like a pesky insect. "It's all for show, Mike. To paint herself a caring human being. She supports ecological causes, quite vocally... but do you think her lavish lifestyle isn't *still* underwritten by the oil money that the Vankemp empire was, and continues to be, built upon?"

I held up a "stop" hand. "I leave such things to you political types. I'm just a working-class capitalist who was hired to find, and deal with, a blackmailer. And with all due respect, sir, you seem to be it."

His expression was somber, even regretful. "I'm not after money, Mike."

"What *are* you after?"

Now his eyes bore down on me, hard and dark and direct. "A simple public announcement from Jamie Winters."

I looked back at him the same way. "You want him to drop out of the presidential race?"

A quick shrug. "Well, he hasn't officially announced yet... but yes. That's exactly what I want." Something proud and yet defensive came into his expression, his chin lifting. *"That* is this reluctant blackmailer's price. What I *require."*

I leaned back, shook my head, gave up half a smile. "The trouble, Governor, is we're talking about a cassette tape—so easily copied. There's really no way for you to assure my clients that you haven't made backups."

The chin stayed up. "You would have my word."

"That would be good enough for me, Governor." I shook my head. "But probably not my clients."

His eyes tightened as he looked past me into his thoughts. Then his gaze swiveled back to me.

"All right," he said. "Suppose I *had* made copies. Suppose I made them even now. If my price has been met—if Jamie Winters makes that statement, and indeed does not make a bid for the Democratic presidential nomination—what further value could that tape possibly have for me? Only a *negative* value—as evidence that I used illegal means to force a rival out of the race."

"But you're telling me you *haven't* made copies."

A confident nod. "I have not. My recourse, should Winters agree to drop out of the race and then not keep his word, would be to seek a qualified investigator… not you, Mike, because that would be a conflict of interest… to look into the senator's extra-marital affairs. My understanding is that his current secretary is only the latest in a long line of such conquests. It would be distasteful to me, but I would see to it that he was properly…"

"Smeared," I said.

He said nothing.

I grunted a laugh. "You'd work through one of the papers, I would imagine. Investigative reporters, political columnists."

"Yes. I still have my media contacts. Do I disappoint you, Mike?" His smile returned, bitter now. "That I would engage in such end-justifies-the-means behavior?"

I shrugged. "I don't think I have a lot of room to bitch in that department, Governor…. I'll make a call."

At the bar I was provided with a phone. I found Senator Winters back at his Flatiron Building office. Lisa Long put me right through.

The bartender was polite enough to stand well away and none of the few customers present, including the governor, were near enough to hear. Still, I was circumspect, and spoke in terms at times that would be vague to anyone but the client I was filling in. I took my time and Winters mostly just listened.

When I'd wrapped it up, Winters said, biting off the words, "That sanctimonious old bastard. Goddamnit!… What do you think I should do, Mike?"

"Well, first talk it over with Nicole, of course. Is she around?"

"She's at the penthouse. I'll call her and see what she says. Damnit!"

"Mr. Winters. Jamie. This political crapola is admittedly not my area of expertise. But as an outsider, I can take a look at you and say, what the hell—you're a young man. Keep your nose clean and go for another senate term, why don't you? Bide your time."

His words were acid-edged: "Hughes is crazy if he thinks a White House bid is in the cards for him."

"So let him try, and fail. You and Nicole close up shop on the open marriage, and keep your eyes on the prize."

"…I'll talk to her. But the old goat *has* to have copies!"

"Actually, I doubt it. I think this whole thing puts a bad taste in his mouth. You postpone your White House urge till after another senate term, and you'll be fine."

"You really think so, Mike?"

What I really thought was we ought to have term limits in this country, but I left that out.

"Yeah," I said. "You can trust him. As far as it goes."

"How far is that?"

"Well, he's a politician. Think it over. Call me when you decide. I'll ask for a couple days to mull it."

"He's still there at the 21 with you?"

"Right. Not listening in, of course. We're lunching. I'm waiting on a solid-gold hamburger."

We said curt goodbyes and hung up.

That burger was just arriving as I sat.

"Jamie and his wife are discussing it," I told the governor. "I said he could have a couple of days. Is that all right?"

"Agreeable," he said with a nod.

The meatloaf-ish burger was tasty, if not twenty-one bucks' worth. It came on grilled Italian bread with a nice side of hand-cut fries. The senator and I concentrated on eating, avoiding the embarrassment of any further talk.

We were just finishing up when the bartender called me back to the phone.

"Take the deal," the senator's voice said.

Damn, that was fast!

I said, "Nicole's on board?"

"Yes."

"You don't sound happy."

"Would you be?"

He hung up.

I went back to the table. The waiter was there. The governor was ordering another round, but I declined another of my "usual." You could accuse 21 of overpricing but not of watering the drinks.

Sitting down again, I said, "You have a clear field, Governor—at least where Senator Winters is concerned. He's decided he's a little too young and unseasoned to go after the big prize just now. He thinks going after a second term in the Senate makes perfect sense."

"Was that your suggestion?"

I nodded. "You two will make a pol out of me yet. After he makes his statement, why don't you deliver that tape to me and I'll get it to my clients."

"Why don't I?" he said, with one of the saddest smiles I've ever seen. He reached into his suit coat pocket and brought out an Ampex cassette tape and laid it on the red-and-white checkered tablecloth like a tip.

I pointed at it, keeping a distance, as if it might bite. "That's the original? Right out of the senator's intercom set-up?"

"That's it," the governor said, nodding. "And, as I said, there are no copies. You don't mind delivering that, do you, Mike?"

"No," I said. "But I think I'll have that drink after all."

CHAPTER EIGHT

Even before *Rosemary's Baby* and John Lennon were shot there, the gothic, nineteenth-century Dakota Building on the Upper West Side looked like something out of a horror show, the kind of monstrosity of a mansion you walked to on a rain-swept dark night when your car broke down and you had no other option. The same was true in the afternoon.

Rumor had it that ghosts, including the late Beatle's, turned up frequently at 72nd Street and Central Park West, but it was better known as a haunt of the rich and famous who were mostly still with us. Lauren Bacall and Leonard Bernstein lived here (not together) and so once had Lillian Gish and Boris Karloff (also not bunkmates). Current residents included Joe Namath, Roberta Flack, and Rudolf Nureyev. Plenty of others, just as rich and famous, had been turned down by the notoriously picky co-op board.

I couldn't have gotten in even on a temporary basis, if I hadn't been expected by a tenant. A cab dropped me at the arched main entry, designed to accommodate horse-drawn carriages. Past the uniformed doorman, in the courtyard of the looming square-shaped building, I took an elevator in the nearest corner and went up to the seventh floor. Surrounded by dark, gloomy woodwork, I made my way to residence 72 and pushed the buzzer.

The door was answered by a guy who was maybe thirty, around five eleven, in a stylish gray suit and a black t-shirt whose athletic build didn't need those shoulder pads, unless a round of touch football was in the offing. As handsome as a guy in a Ralph Lauren ad, his chin dimpled, his complexion olive, he wore his black hair fairly long and slicked back. But his most distinguishing feature was a flattened nose that indicated somewhere in his past—collegiate probably—there had been boxing.

"Mike Hammer," I said, "for Nicole Winters. I'm expected."

He nodded politely, said, "Yes, Mr. Hammer," and stepped aside, gesturing me in. He took my hat and coat and hung them in a closet, then led the way down a long entry corridor.

He glanced back. "I'm Andrew Morrow, Ms. Winters' secretary." His voice was mellow and mid-pitched. He glanced back with a smile, adding, "Actually, I work for the Nicole Vankemp Foundation."

"The umbrella for her various charitable endeavors, I assume."

"That's right, Mr. Hammer."

We entered into a sun-streaming, airy, ivory-drenched loft-like endless living room with a wet bar, a white baby grand piano, and a twelve-foot ceiling, easy. The sidewall was mirrored, like a ballet studio, making the impressive space seem even more vast, the floor's oak sanded to a near bone, the whiteness of the room offset slightly by carved mahogany. At the far and near end of the staggering space were fireplaces original to the room, their fancy woodwork washed white, and over their respective mantels hung big-framed images—a blue-dominated Marilyn by Warhol and a Roy Lichtenstein comic-book panel of a redheaded woman talking into a phone.

The result was a vintage area turned modern, the furnishings metallic with colorful pop-art cushions, red, blue, yellow, green. On the red-cushioned couch, before a glass-and-steel coffee table between her and the tall windows onto the park, sat Nicole in an emerald jumpsuit. The redheaded beauty was leaning forward, leafing through oversize photographs of nightclub interiors.

She glanced up at me with a smile, her lipstick a shade similar to her hair, which was ponytailed back. With no preamble, she said, "I'm just looking over some venues in Miami. We're doing a cancer fund-raiser down there in a few months."

"For or against?"

That stopped her for a moment, then she laughed and it had a nice musical quality. "You're a very bad man, Mike."

"So I hear."

The male secretary was at my side and Nicole looked up at us and nodded toward him. "I see you've met Andrew—my majordomo."

"We've met." I threw him a smile. "What does a majordomo do in this day and age?"

Andrew frowned a little, wondering if he should answer. Nicole relieved him of the chore.

"Well, right now," she said, and gestured to a spiral pad on the glass coffee-table top, just to one side of the nightclub photos, "he's been taking dictation. Something like a dozen letters today— people wanting help, people wanting money." She shrugged. "We do what we can."

Andrew collected his spiral pad and said to her, "Would you like me to run those errands now, Ms. Winters?"

"Yes, would you please, Andrew?" she asked brightly.

He gave her a half-bow, then smiled tightly and gave me a quarter of one. He went back the way we'd come. I heard a closet door open, and the sound of him climbing into a topcoat, then the front door opened and closed.

She patted the cushion next to her. "Alone at last."

I sat. "What sort of errands?"

She flipped a hand. "Oh, banking. Arranging for us to have flowers at an event coming up. A banquet at the Waldorf with details that need tending. A hundred things."

"He doesn't look it."

"Look what?"

"Gay."

The musical laugh again. "Well, he's not. He's quite hetero. Not that you can tell just looking at a person." She shook her head and the ponytail swung. "What an amusingly Cro-Magnon way of looking at things you have, Mike."

"Is that what I have? Frankly, with that boxer's nose and fullback's build, I figured he might be security."

She nodded. "Well, actually to a degree he is. Andrew wears several hats, Mike, and I don't mean fedoras. He handles much of the actual work that my foundation requires, and he acts as our in-house security. Also, he's a sort of bodyguard who goes almost everywhere with me."

"He's live-in, then?"

"Yes. This is a sizeable condo, Mike. Front to back, this living room space alone is 3,500 feet. Andrew has a room off the kitchen, and comes and goes through the service entrance. Are you wondering if he's also my boy toy?"

I grinned at her. "I hadn't got that far. But it might be convenient having that in-house, too."

She pursed her lips in a wry smile and patted my leg. "I'm sorry to disappoint you, Mike, but my husband takes care of that kind of thing around here when I'm so inclined, or is that reclined? The open arrangement Jamie and I've enjoyed these last few years doesn't preclude enjoying each *other* as well.... Would you like a drink? Your usual?"

She knew what my usual was, too, even if this was my first time here.

"No, I had a late lunch," I said, "and it included three cocktails."

"That's right. Jamie said you were at 21, meeting with the ex-governor." The ponytail swung again. "What a *surprise* that was! That stuffy old goat, a blackmailer! Still waters *do* run deep."

"How do you think your husband will take having to give up his presidential bid?"

Her eyebrows went up and down. "Oh, he'll take it hard. But I'm not so sure waiting till he's a little older, and has been in office a while, isn't such a bad thing.... Nothing I can get you?"

I shrugged. "If you have coffee, I'd take it."

"I could use some myself. Black, I assume?"

"No. Cream and sugar. I like it sweet."

"I bet you do." She got up and padded off, the emerald jumpsuit designed to be loose on the legs but to hug her bottom, which was worth hugging. Her feet were bare.

While she was gone—fetching coffee in this place was like going on safari—I got up, skirted the glass-and-steel table and went over to the many windows onto the world. And the world was mostly Central Park.

Autumn had set the park on fire with orange and red, a dazzling display of shades and shimmer as wind riffled through. Here, in the midst of a town that had so much ugliness in it, was the beauty of nature, a reminder of what this hunk of real estate had been before we screwed the Indians out of it. Of course if you walked through all that nature at night, you could still get scalped. Ugliness likes to conceal itself in beauty.

Nicole returned with a little deco silver service with two cups, a coffee pot, matching sugar bowl and lidded creamer. This she set on the glass-top table and poured herself a cup and then me.

"I didn't want to guess," she said, indicating the sugar and cream.

I fixed up my own cup, not sparing either of the add-ons, and she smiled and said, "You *are* a sissy."

"Flaming," I said, and sipped. Perfect.

She leaned back and did some sipping herself. Put her bare feet and their orange-red toenails on the glass table-top. She was looking out toward the park and its fall colors, or so I thought— really she was dipping into her thoughts.

"Andrew is a special young man," she said, musingly. "He was a good friend of my late brother's. David? Davie was a troubled soul, I'm afraid." She swallowed. "He was driving when…"

I'd read about it in the papers, several years ago, but nothing had brought it to mind in these circumstances till now. "Your brother had several drunk driving arrests, I recall. Didn't have a license when he crashed."

She frowned over at me. I guess I sounded callous.

"Andrew was in the car with him," she said in a measured way. "He was badly injured, a broken leg, broken arm. Needed some facial reconstruction. We took care of him. Now he takes care of us."

"Was he in college with your brother?"

She sipped coffee, nodded. "They were at Cornell. David was studying law, Andrew business. After David's death, Andrew finished up and we hired him."

"A security man with those kinds of injuries?"

Nicole waved that off. "Oh, Andrew is one hundred percent. He was an absolute *star* at physical therapy." She shrugged. "He was a boxing champ at Cornell. On scholarship."

"Doesn't come from your kind of background, though."

"No." She gave me half a smile; it was prettier than most women's whole ones. "Do I strike you as a snob, Mike?"

I shook my head. "No. I know you've had your share of tragedy. I read the papers. Your mother committed suicide when you were small. You have a sister in Europe who I gather you haven't spoken to in years. Your father died fairly young. Being heir to a fortune doesn't buy anybody out of misfortune."

"Not a snob, then."

"Not that I can tell. I did describe you as a spoiled brat to our ex-governor, though."

She beamed. "Ha! I suppose that's right. How can anyone swimming in my kind of money be anything else?"

"Well, at least you haven't drowned in it." I shrugged. "You get points for trying to use your wealth, your fame, for good."

Nicole looked at me searchingly, as if there might be sarcasm or irony or judgment in my words. She couldn't find any because there weren't any to find.

Very quietly, she said, "Thank you, Mike."

She placed her coffee cup on the glass table-top. She sat back, tucked her legs under her, arms winged out along the couch cushions behind her. The hair and lipstick and painted toenails seemed almost too perfectly matched. Was she really a redhead, or was that just another fashion statement?

I drank my coffee. "Nice little pad. These studio apartments are great."

That amused her. "Used to be Judy Garland's place. Yoko Ono lives next door. I can hear her making music through the walls."

"The management ought to give you a discount."

That amused her, too, but then she leaned toward me and said, "So… do you have it with you?"

"Yup."

Her eyes glittered like a kid on Christmas morning contemplating a real haul. "Do I need to round up a cassette player?"

"No. I stopped by my office and picked up one of ours, in case you wanted to check it." I dug in my pocket for the small metal tape player, the cassette already in it. "Would you like me to leave this for you?"

She was looking at the little metal-case tape player that filled the palm of my hand. "No. I want to hear."

I held up the gadget between my thumb and middle finger. "I haven't listened to it myself. I didn't think that was my place. So if this turns out to be the ex-governor's voice telling us all to take a flying leap, I can't be held responsible."

"Understood. I want to hear." Her eyes still had a strange sparkle and she was smiling. Anticipating.

That struck me as damn odd, but I put the tape player on the glass table-top and punched PLAY. It began in the middle of things.

"*There,*" Lisa Long's voice said. "*Right there! Oh! Oh!… Ooooooh!… That's so good… You're so good…*"

A rustle of clothing. A zipper. More cloth rustle.

Now came the senator's voice: "*My God… oh my God… baby, that is sooooo sweet… deeper…deeper!*"

I said to Nicole, "Why don't I fast-forward, and make sure that—"

"No!" She gripped my wrist as my hand reached out. "No, Mike… Let it play."

She was listening intently, her breath coming fast.

So I just sat there, as the sounds of foreplay melded into lovemaking, interrupted only by further rustles of clothing being removed. The screak of flesh rubbing rhythmically against leather and the squeak of cushions defined the co-starring presence of the couch in that inner office. Moans of delight and ever-heavier breathing, male and female, built into the expected grunts and gasps, and finally the female cry of, "*You're going to make me… you're going to make me! Give it to me! Yes! Yes!*"

I admit it. I was embarrassed. You might think it would have been exciting, but I was only ill at ease, sitting next to a woman whose husband was making passionate love to another woman. Even if they did have an open marriage, it unsettled me. Something like guilt… no, not something *like* guilt, but guilt *itself*… flooded through me as I thought of how often in our own "open" days I had taken advantage of Velda's willingness to put up with my randy damn nature and wild-oats-sowing ways and wait until I was ready to commit to her entirely.

Then something happened that challenged all those noble yet shabby thoughts.

The tape shut itself off after perhaps a minute of nothing at all. The beautiful woman next to me was sitting with her head back, her eyes lidded, her breath slow and heavy now.

"That's the original," I said, in a business-like way, "if the governor is to be believed. And I do believe him."

She just looked at me. It was the look a lioness gives a cornered wild hog. She walked around the sofa, slow, graceful, almost purring, and planted herself a few yards away. I craned to look at her. What the hell...?

She stood with her legs apart, like the statue of an Amazon goddess. The emerald jumpsuit had a zipper from the throat to the waist. She used it. Slowly. The sound of the zipper inching its way down was like a growl. Then her hands simultaneously found the shoulders of the garment and she let it down to bunch around her waist. Her full breasts had large pale, pink nipples, the aureoles blending in with her lightly freckled flesh. No tanning bed for her. No sunning on vacation. She reached behind her, her breasts staying full as they rose, and undid her ponytail and let her hair loose, like a horse shaking its mane. Then she stood straight, legs together now, as her hands tugged down the rest of the garment and she stepped out of the emerald pile of cloth, kicked it away with an orange-red-nailed foot, then resumed her legs-apart stance as a goddess of Everything Woman.

She was a real redhead all right.

That was as fiery a bush as anything autumn in Central Park had to offer. The mirrored wall behind her revealed a bottom full and rounded and dimpled, as creamy as the cream in my coffee.

Her arms reached out, her smile a summoning sneer, her fingers of both her hands curling toward me in invitation.

In command.

I got up and came around the couch to her. She smiled as she saw what she had done to me.

I went to her and she pressed herself to me. My right hand found the slope of her back and followed it down as it dipped then rose into full supple smoothness. My other hand cupped one full breast, the nipple taut now. Then her face moved toward mine, lips wet and parted.

I kissed the tip of her nose and backed away.

"You're about ten years too late, honey," I said.

She came forward fast and her arms hugged me and one leg came around and locked me to her. "You heard what he was doing to her on that tape. I want to get even! Isn't that what Mike Hammer does? *Get even?*"

"Doll, nobody ever said Mike Hammer screwed a client. And I don't intend to start now."

She shoved me away, disgusted, and walked around the couch to the coffee table, naked and not giving a damn.

"Don't forget your tape player," she said. "My next listen is going to be on a high-end stereo system."

I went over there to collect my property just as she ejected the tape from it. She took the cassette out and frowned at it.

"This is an Ampex tape," she said, studying it, still frowning.

"So?"

"So it's not the brand they use at my husband's office. That's Maxell."

We looked at each other. My erection was history and her nakedness a non-issue.

"So it's a copy," I said.

Her sneering smile wasn't sexy this time. "So much for your honest ex-governor."

"I'm not so sure. It might be somebody else."

She frowned. "Somebody else... who what?"

"Somebody else," I said, "who has the original."

CHAPTER NINE

The next day found gray massing clouds hovering over the city like giant wads of soggy dirty cotton, just waiting to wring themselves out. You could smell the rain wanting to happen, but the temperature was chill enough now that maybe it would be the icy variety or perhaps one of those crazy storms where it sleets and snows and thunders and lightnings all at once.

Velda and I had spent yesterday evening in her apartment, comparing notes over take-out Chinese and later in front of a fire by her couch. If you think I didn't tell her about the distaff half of our client couple stripping down and baring her burning bush, you don't know me very well. Or Velda either. She got mad. And I got even.

Hadn't Nicole said that was what I was famous for?

But this morning I hadn't gone right into the office. Velda did, to watch the phone and keep things humming. Me, I was calling on ex-governor Harry Hughes and not at 21, either, though the digs today would be fancy enough. I had called ahead, first thing, and Governor Hughes was expecting me at his apartment on one of the upper, residential floors of the Waldorf Astoria.

A light bagels-and-cream-cheese breakfast was awaiting me in the formal dining room of the suite, which also included a long marble-floored living room with matching marble fireplace (a portrait of the governor's late wife over it, no Warhol or pop-art piece here), several bedrooms and a small but complete kitchen. The governor lived alone—no majordomo for errands or protection, either—and answered the door himself. He enjoyed cooking, he said, but often availed himself of room service, particularly for breakfast, like today.

The governor was in a maroon silk robe with black velvet lapels, seated at the head of the table, slathering cream cheese on his lightly toasted bagel. I was buttering mine. We'd had orange juice and were on to coffee.

"Mike," he said, after chewing and swallowing a bite, "I give you my word that I did not make any copies of that tape. I didn't even listen to much of it, just ascertained it was what I'd been told. It… well, this kind of thing is not what I generally traffic in." He shuddered. "I'm not proud of myself for stooping so low."

I shrugged, nibbled buttered bagel. "Governor, I can only tell you that I have it on solid authority that the tape is a copy."

He frowned. "Was there some electronic way you could determine as much?"

"No. It has to do with the brand of tape. It's not what's regularly used at the senator's office."

My distinguished host shook his head of silver-streaked black hair, but not a strand came loose. "All I can say, Mike, is that the Licata boy came around a few days ago, and told me how his 'woman,' as he put it, had come to have the damned thing. That she was on the cleaning staff at the Flatiron, and happened upon it quite accidentally."

That was almost true.

I said, "Licata just dropped by? Didn't phone you first?"

"No. He wouldn't have my number."

Actually, Licata had the governor's number, all right.

"But," Hughes continued, "he knew where I lived because he was a bartender at a get-together I threw here earlier this year. That was how we came to converse, since he was here early and stayed late, and I was his employer for the event."

"Who provided him?"

"It was done through the hotel here." He turned over a hand. "I chatted with Licata at some length, before and after that event, as he was setting up and tearing down. I'm interested in what the real people are doing, you know, what it takes for them to make their way in this modern world. Meaning no condescension, what I'm talking about here is the common man."

"Well, Licata seems to be trying to make *his* way by blackmailing the uncommon man."

The square face with all that character carved in it turned somber, the flesh as gray now as the morning out there. He put down the bagel, as if he'd suddenly lost his appetite.

"And that's what we have in common, Mr. Licata and I," he said, "isn't it? We're both blackmailers. Isn't that what you're implying, Mike?"

I chewed bagel, swallowed the bite, shrugged. "I'm not implying anything. It's a fact. What did he tell you, when you two connected before and after your cocktail party? How he hopes to get married? And better himself? Live someplace where the can isn't down the hall and he and his honey don't have to share it with recovering addicts and welfare cases?"

My host said nothing. His face looked cold, even coldly angry, but I could see the regret, even the shame, swimming in the dark eyes. Maybe that anger was turned inward.

Finally he said, quietly, "The young man's stated ambition was a shabby little thing, by most standards. How he hopes to own a bar of his own there in Brooklyn." He laughed humorlessly. "How very *small* the American dream can sometimes manifest itself."

"And what big nightmares can follow, when you're willing to do anything to pursue it. How much did you pay him?"

"...Five thousand dollars. In cash."

"Small is right. That was a bargain rate. Or it would have been, if that really had been the original of the tape."

Hughes gestured around him. He'd brought some of his own furniture in, apparently—a cabinet filled with china and silver looked heirloom.

"We're alone here, Mike. If you think I'm lying... if you think somewhere I have a box of duplicates of that foul recording... take a look around. Or if I have it squirreled away in a safe deposit box or one of my homes, you'd be free right here and now to try to beat the truth out of me. There was a time when you couldn't have, but you're ten years younger than me and look to be quite physically fit for your age. Isn't that what Mike Hammer is known for? Slapping people around?"

I shook my head. Slapped some more butter on my bagel. "No, I believe you, Governor. But you have a problem. With that tape an obvious copy, there's no reason for Jamie Winters to cooperate with you. Don't expect him to announce he's decided not to pursue the Oval Office. Not with the original and other copies running around out there, impossible to contain."

He sat forward. "In that case, Mike, wouldn't he be ruined eventually, anyway? Wouldn't his presidential hopes be dashed? Leaving him to serve out his senate term in disgrace?"

"Possibly. He might pay Licata and any other blackmailers off—he and his wife could certainly afford it. But your hopes may be dashed as well."

"And why would that be?"

"If the senator is disgraced by the sex scandal, nothing would stop him from going to the police and ruining what's left of your reputation. Ending your career in prison would make a hell of a last chapter for the next volume of your autobiography, Governor. You'd just have to work hard at not dying behind bars, or else you wouldn't get to enjoy the royalties."

Suddenly that famous face smiled at me. The only sound was the bite of bagel I was working on.

"Do you have a suggestion, Mike? Or are you just sitting in judgment? I remember that notorious newspaper headline, all those years ago—*'I, the Jury,' Says Mike Hammer.* You avenged a fellow soldier. Now you want to humiliate another."

I used a napkin on my mouth and hands. "Yeah, how the mighty have fallen and all that shit. Look, I do have a suggestion."

"I'm listening."

"Hire me to get your money back from Mr. Tony Licata. I can tell him that you are prepared to go public about the tape he sold you, unless he returns your money and hands over the original—and any copies—to me. That just might make him cooperate. And satisfy my clients."

His eyes tightened with consideration. "But it couldn't be a bluff."

"No. You couldn't be bluffing. Of course, if Licata calls what he *thinks* is your bluff, and you have to come clean? We could maybe spin it a little—isn't that what you political types are expert at? Spin?"

A trace of amusement flickered on thin lips. "How would *you* spin this, Mike?"

I shrugged. "I would get my clients to say you didn't try to blackmail them. That in fact you tried to help them. You would say your intent was not to blackmail anybody, but to acquire this damning tape to prevent just such a thing."

He frowned in doubt. "Your clients would go along with this?"

"I think so."

"But that would mean exposing the tape…"

I shrugged. "Not if I really do lay hands on the original and the duplicates first. And destroy them. Also, I still have a few media contacts of my own who remember my name. Who would spread the rumor that the tape was a phony, something Licata and his girlfriend cooked up."

He gave me a sideways look that emphasized that shovel jaw of his. "It's dangerous."

"It got dangerous the moment you thought blackmail was an option you could justify. What do you say, Governor? Shall we give it a try?"

He held the thought in like a deep breath underwater. Then he exploded: "Yes! Yes!" He banged a fist on the table and rattled the breakfast dishes. "Let's see if we can clean up after my own foolish mistake. You need a retainer, I trust?"

I pushed away from the table and stood. "If I pull this off, you can send five thousand bucks to the Nicole Vankemp Foundation. She's got the morals of an alley cat, but it'd be fitting if some good cause she helps gets a boost out of this."

The dark eyes narrowed as he gazed up at me. "What do you get out of it, Mike? Or are you just a good citizen?"

"I'm on a $10,000 retainer, Governor. I can afford to be generous."

The gray sky escorted me on my second excursion to Brooklyn in two days. The clouds were tumbling, somersaulting, nasty billowing stuff that might have been pouring out of a burning building. Occasionally came a rumbling, like God was hungry and looking to make a meal of the pitiful creatures moving on their pointless way below. The cold that went with that grumble was a clammy thing, like a dead man's handshake, but when I turned the heat on in the Ford, it got hot too quick, and when I turned it back off, the cold came back right away. No "just right" for Goldilocks or the rest of humanity.

Traffic was in a bad mood, too, and the Ford seemed to make every car and driver around us mad, horns honking at us for just being alive. Any urge to give the other guy an "Up yours!" went away when you saw the foul dark glares and knew maybe you'd get shot for expressing your opinion.

Finally, on Park Slope's Fifth Avenue, where the graffiti couldn't agree whether smack was heaven or hell, the sky exploded and what came down were pellets of hail, a furious sky wielding its machine gun with a madman's indiscretion.

When I pulled over in front of the once-proud four-story brownstone on Seventh Avenue, I had to sit there for five minutes before the hail let up, watching little balls bounce off the hood of the Ford, hoping they wouldn't leave dents, listening to their tuneless tap-dancing on the roof. The coldness did not stop my breath from fogging up the windshield and my turned-up trenchcoat collars didn't provide enough warmth to stop my teeth from chattering.

Then the attack was over, and I climbed out, the brown grass of adjacent front yards littered with little white pellets, like a truck hauling mothballs had backed up and dumped its load. My feet crunched as I went up the walk and climbed the steps to the modest stoop and banged my fist on the door.

It jarred open.

I pushed it the rest of the way and was about to call out to the landlady when I saw her fallen form on the kitchen floor down at the end of the hallway that hugged the second-floor stairway. I shrugged out of the damp trenchcoat and shed it like a snake from its skin and moved quietly and quickly toward the kitchen, my hand filling itself with the .45 from under my unbuttoned suit coat, the weapon with its walnut grips completing my fist.

The old gal had been clobbered a good one, from behind, her white perm smudged scarlet in back. I knelt and checked her pulse at her wrist.

Nothing.

At her throat.

Nothing.

She was facedown in a kitchen that smelled of corned beef and cabbage again, a pot of the stuff simmering on a Depression-era green-and-white stove that was about a decade away from an antique shop. The boarders were getting leftovers today, but they would have to serve themselves. Their landlady was dead.

So now it was murder.

Blackmail got my business, but murder made me mad.

A phone on the kitchen wall had a posted list of emergency numbers and I considered using the one for the cops. But the old landlady was in no hurry, and it occurred to me to check a certain apartment first. I went up the stairs, as quietly as possible, which wasn't very damn quiet, gum soles doing little to fight the creaking. When I got to the top, tragic faces peeked out of cracked doors and I waved them back and the doors closed reflexively.

The door to 2A was shut but not locked and I opened it slowly, then went in fast and low, the .45 moving right to left and back again.

Silence greeted me and an all-too-familiar scent—acrid-edged copper, the scorched aftermath of gunfire mingled with the odor of spilled blood. With my left hand I shut the door softly behind me, already mesmerized by the sight of the woman on the floor, right there in front of me. Maybe she'd been running for it.

She didn't make it.

What a good-looking woman the Flatiron cleaning gal had been not long ago, a redhead like Nicole Winters, her pale flesh lightly freckled, and a lot of it showing. She was in that same green satin robe as the day before, sprawled on the floor in the midst of all that mismatched secondhand-looking furniture, the garment flung wide open with a cream-colored bra and sheer panties all that separated her nudity from prying eyes.

Erin Dunn was done, all right, a corpse on her back in a position a living person couldn't assume for long, a twisted prone posture, legs going left, upper torso twisting right, one arm reaching for nothing, the other's angle like a broken hinge, while sightless sky-blue eyes stared at a ceiling she could not see, not with the top of her head blown off, mid-forehead up, in a scattering of bone chunks and brain lumps painted as red by blood as the pool of the stuff they waded in, her hair fanned out in the crimson mini-lake like ghastly seaweed.

I kept low as I moved across the sitting area into the bedroom, its door open, thinking whoever did this might still be here. The corpse was fresh enough, the blood out there wet and shimmering, and maybe the cops were on the way already. A big gun had done this, probably as big as my .45, and even in the hailstorm some resident must have heard its mechanical thunder. But no tenant in this place had a phone, and the landlady hadn't made a call, that was for damn sure.

Nor had any of those frightened faces come out of their hidey holes, not even to flee.

The sky roared, laughing at me, but no rain or hail followed, nothing battering the windows but wind-driven branches. So the silence wasn't silence at all, not when you really listened, and that was when I heard the moaning.

He was on the other side of the bed, on the floor, on his back where I couldn't see him from the doorway. The room didn't have much in it—a double bed that looked like something a motel had thrown out, a couple of dressers that didn't have anything to do with each other, this one maple and modern, that one walnut and Victorian.

And, also, a man named Tony Licata, down there on his back in his wife-beater t-shirt and jockey shorts and black socks, like in the smoker flicks. He was home from the hospital, but he looked pretty damn sick with that red-bubbling mouth and that belly wound and his bloody hands gripping himself, trying to hold the pain and his intestines in. His darkly handsome face wasn't dark at all now—it was as white as a fresh pair of gym togs, but the only exercise Tony was getting was dying slowly.

I knelt and asked, "Who did this to you, Tony?"

But he couldn't answer through the bubbling froth. His eyes beseeched me but there was nothing I could do for him. Oh, I could have told him I'd get him an ambulance, and one would come for him, all right, but he'd be making his exit in a body bag. Or I could have put one between his eyes, but I didn't care to answer for that. I shook my head. My expression told him to make his peace while he had time.

The only other room in the excuse for an apartment was that half a kitchen. The counter was clean and the sink was empty— Erin Dunn ran a tidy ship. A back way out had an open door onto old weather-beaten stairs that were covered in melting hailstones. The hailstones didn't show signs of anyone going down those stairs recently enough to turn them into crushed ice. That probably meant the killer had gone out this way before the sky spewed hail, a storm that hadn't lasted more than five minutes.

Whoever did this was gone.

Maybe a neighbor saw the killer exit, either out the front or probably this back way, with the door standing open like it was. I'd tell the cops when they came and they could canvass the neighborhood. Of course what I should really do now was go down and step over the landlady's corpse and use that list of emergency numbers on the wall to make the phone call to the Brooklyn PD.

What I did instead was start searching the place. I got my gloves on and started with the bedroom. Neither of the dressers had anything but clothes in them, one her stuff, the other his. A scuffed-up bedside table had a drawer with nothing special in, the usual junk, tissues, smokes, fingernail clippers, a romance paperback. Certainly not a Maxwell cassette tape, much less a box of duplicate tapes.

But I was sure that the soon-to-be-late Licata had the original, that selling a copy to the governor had only been one of the ways he had in mind to get rich off that sex tape, or anyway buy that dream saloon of his. The killer had come in, knocked out the old lady and headed upstairs and somehow got into the apartment. Maybe just knocked and the door opened a crack and he forced himself the rest of the way in. Or maybe talked his way in.

What a sloppy, reckless endeavor, though!

If the killer knew anything about this situation, he or she could have at least waited till Erin Dunn was at work. If it had been me after the tape, I'd have done this in the middle of the night and either beaten the thing out of Licata, or taken him down in his sleep, knocked him out or chloroformed him or some damn thing.

And searched the place at my leisure. Found the tapes, and if I didn't find them, go back to Licata and get it out of him any way I could.

Or ideally, if there was a time when Licata was at his bartending job while the Dunn woman was in the city at her job, nobody at all would have to be rousted, let alone killed. You could sneak in that back way and not even deal with the landlady. Search the place and, if you didn't find anything, wait for Licata to come home and only then beat it out of him.

That's how I'd have done it.

But this fool had blundered in while they both were here, and wound up shooting them both... then what? Skedaddled without making a search? I didn't see any sign that the place had been tossed. What the hell was going on?

There was another nightstand, mismatching of course, and it too had plenty of junk, Kleenex pack, pencils, a pack of Trojans, books of matches, half a pack of Camels. But tucked in back was a little Saturday Night Special, a .38 snub, which might've turned things around if Tony had got to it. Just ask Tony. Only you couldn't. He was down there on the floor, unconscious, his mouth not bubbling anymore. Dead now. Lucky to be. Getting gut-shot is one of the worst ways to buy it.

I went over to the closet, opened the door, and from the darkness somebody jumped out at me.

Somebody who had just shot these two, and had heard me come in, probably already in the bedroom, and ducked in the closet and waited for me to run out and call for help.

But instead I'd poked around. Later it would amuse me to think of the guy stuck in that closet, not knowing what the hell to do, while I rustled through the place. It would also occur to me later that I was lucky a guy who'd just killed two unarmed people hadn't gone ahead and burst out and put a round or two into me. Gut-shot *me*, maybe.

Right now, though, I was dealing with taking a hard straight-arm to my chest, knocking me back, then two hands—one clutching a big automatic with a bulky noise-suppressor on its snout— shoving me on the floor onto my back. I was clawing at my coat for the .45 when he kicked me in the head and leapt over me like the obstruction I'd become.

I should have been unconscious, but I wasn't. The pain consumed my brain the way an auditorium gets filled by a philharmonic orchestra, but this was a discordant symphony and all my motor skills weren't playing any song at all. Yet somehow my eyes managed to see. He was in black, all in black, including a balaclava that made a nonentity of him. He scurried awkwardly for the door, then turned and pointed the bulky-looking automatic at me, eye holes in the black woolen mask showing wide dark eyes, with white all around, that stared at me unblinking.

Even with my head a ringing, screaming thing, I knew this was the end. Finally all of it was catching up to me. I saw Velda's face and she was beautiful and smiling and then in an instant she was gone, replaced by the faces of men I'd killed, laughing at me, this one merging into the next, and every laugh made the pain in my skull throb and then the bastard's gun jammed and he was gone.

CHAPTER TEN

The roiling clouds had smoothed themselves out into a vast gray ceiling, but the threat of rain still made itself felt in air you could have swum through.

The bodies had been carted off, the morgue wagon gone, while inside the brownstone, lab techs were still dusting and photographing. I was out front behind the wheel of my parked Ford with the engine going and the motor running, the heat on. Another kind of heat was seated beside me in the passenger seat: Detective Earl Brice of the Brooklyn Borough Homicide Squad.

Brice, black, maybe thirty-five, had a tamed Afro and a trimmed Shaft mustache to go with a handsomely carved face. He was in a tan raincoat over a sharp charcoal suit with a black-and-white striped tie. He'd been pro all the way, so far, but he stopped short of being friendly.

"You could have a serious concussion," he said, his tone thick but his articulation crisp.

"I've had concussions before," I said. "I can tell a bad one." I shrugged. "I carry aspirin and I took four. There's a doctor in my building back in the city. He'll check me. Let's get this over with."

His eyes took me in quickly, then looked straight ahead. "We've never met, have we?"

"No."

"Does it surprise you I've heard of you?"

"A little. You're young. And I keep a low profile these days."

Another quick look. "Three dead bodies is a low profile?"

I shrugged again. "I didn't make them dead. Look, I get along with most of you guys. I'm tight with Captain Chambers at One Police Plaza. Check with him."

He was staring out the windshield at a squad car. Uniform officers were milling on the sidewalk nearby. They were joking and laughing, nothing really inappropriate—just evidence that violent death was nothing new around here.

"You waited over half an hour to call this in," Brice reminded me.

"I got kicked in the head. I sat down and gathered myself and when my noggin felt up to it, I went down and used the phone."

"But you don't need a trip to the ER."

"No. I told you. I—"

"Right. You took four aspirin. Okay. Let's take another run at this."

My smile was as pleasant as it was insincere. "Sure. I came out here to your sunny borough to talk to the Dunn woman and this Tony Licata, her live-in boyfriend. She worked in the city at the Flatiron Building, nights, part of the cleaning service that handles the place. My client has an office there. Something was taken from that office—stolen—and so Dunn needed an interview. I gave it to her."

"Yesterday."

"Right. And I came back today with some follow-up."

"Follow-up about what, Mr. Hammer?"

"We can get into that if it becomes necessary. And, no, the robbery wasn't reported. As I explained, I work for an attorney. The client is technically his, which takes us into areas of attorney/client privilege."

The look he gave me wasn't so quick this time. "That doesn't cover the *identity* of the client."

"You'll have to talk to the attorney in question. I've already provided his contact information."

The detective sighed. "What's your take on this, Mr. Hammer? You've worked an unusual number of homicides for a private investigator."

"Well, it's kind of a specialty." I smiled at him some more, trying to make him stop looking out the windshield and make some eye contact. "Do you have a low opinion of people in my trade?"

"Not necessarily."

"Wouldn't blame you if you did, Detective Brice. It can be a filthy way to make a buck, if it's about divorce or skip tracing and such. But for all the homicides I've been involved with... all of the self-defense pleas, which is probably why you've heard about me... I still have my license. I'm still in demand with the top insurance companies. No other private inquiry agency in New York as small as mine does as much big business."

That got a dryly amused smile going under that Richard Roundtree mustache. "Fame is the name of the game, huh, Hammer?"

The "Mister" had disappeared suddenly.

"I'm fine with giving you my take on this thing," I said. "But you go first."

He was still looking straight out the windshield. We hadn't yet made much eye contact. I couldn't tell if what he was holding in was contempt or respect or maybe just a general weariness that came with working the homicide beat.

"I can tell you how my boss is going to read it," he said, "without him ever setting foot at the crime scene. He's going to say it's a typical case of some junkie looking for money or swag."

"But that's not what *you* think."

Now he looked at me. Really looked. The eyes were as black as his hair and his mustache, and those eyes knew how to convey cool and heat all at once. "No. And it's probably not what *you* think went down either, Hammer. And I'll tell you why."

"Please."

Eyes on the brownstone now. "This was premeditated. Somebody came to the door, the old landlady answered, that somebody forced his way in… or maybe *her* way in, probably his, though… and the old girl got scared and ran down the hall and got chased and whacked on the head in the kitchen. Whacked, *period*, hard as she got hit."

I nodded.

"Then he or she, but probably he—"

I raised a palm. "A 'he' jumped me. You can stop hedging."

Brice nodded. "He went upstairs to a specific apartment. There are three floors of apartments to choose from, and four apartments per floor. Each floor only has one of the 'larger' apartments, which is two rooms and a kitchenette. The others are single-room affairs. And the intruder knew which room on what floor to hit."

"Could have been luck."

A rare grin flashed under the black mustache. "Could be I'll win the lottery, but I don't think so. You said he had a silencer on that piece."

"He did. That's illegal in this state."

"So is killing three people, Hammer. Junkies on the prowl, lookin' to feed their habit, don't use noise suppressors. If they had one of those—"

"They'd hock it," I said with a smile.

He smiled a little at that. Nodded again. "This was somebody prepared to kill. Possibly *intending* to kill. If he was searching for something, he likely did it after the kills. The place wasn't torn apart like a druggie on a wild-ass hunt for cash or valuables."

Silence. For maybe a minute that silence was broken only by a distant siren and the chatting and laughing of the two uniformed cops at their post.

I said, "I could offer a scenario."

"Why don't you?"

"The old lady was a real piece of work. He probably figured he could talk his way past her, but that didn't pan out. So he ended up pushing his way in and chasing her into the kitchen and cracking her head like an egg."

Brice nodded, real slow.

I said, "She was fixing lunch for the boarders. The killer knew this was a boarding house and the pot on the stove with enough to feed everybody in the place would tell him that the old broad would be discovered soon enough. Probably within half an hour, an hour at the outside."

"What's your point?"

"Well, a junkie might have panicked and split. But the killer goes on up and takes care of business. I don't think he expected the boyfriend to be home. Licata would likely have been at work. But he was in the hospital the day before, maybe overnight and just got home, and was taking it easy today."

Brice's eyes narrowed. "Go on. I'm with you."

"So the killer waves the gun at the Dunn woman and says, 'Where is it?' and she tells him it's in the bedroom, whatever it is he's after. When the killer goes in the bedroom, she makes a break for it and he hears and sees and shoots her. Licata in the bedroom maybe tries to hide or go for that little gun in the nightstand, but he doesn't get it. Instead *he* gets shot, too. Two in the belly."

"Yeah." Brice shuddered a little. "Slow fuckin' death."

"Not my choice of an exit, either. For me, I mean. For certain people, I'm fine with it. Where was I?"

"The killer is alone in an apartment with two corpses and a ticking clock by way of a dead landlady downstairs."

"Right," I said. "So what does he do? Split the hell out of there, 'cause everything has gone tits up? No. He calmly searches the place. Doesn't toss it, but methodically looks for a specific item or items. It's not a tough place to search, but since he's in the bedroom, he starts with the two dressers. He finds jack shit. So he starts on the closet, and then some damn fool comes in."

"You."

"Me. Possibly he glimpses me, and sees I have a gun in my mitt. He ducks in the closet. I come in and have a look around and he waits. If I look in the closet, he's ready for me."

"And you look in the closet."

"I do."

"And get jumped and kicked in the head and close to shot."

"Close only counts in horseshoes."

"One last question, Hammer."

"Yeah?"

"When he pointed that silenced rod at you?"

"Yeah?"

"Why didn't you crap your pants?"

I grinned. "I was busy having my life pass in front of my eyes."

Detective Brice took all of my contact information and shook me loose. On Fifth Avenue, I pulled over and stopped near the phone booth that I used the day before and used it again, calling Velda at the office.

I filled her in.

"You're determined to get yourself killed," she said as I wrapped it up, "before you make an honest woman out of me."

"It's the only way out left to me, doll. Look, before I called it in, I gave that apartment a thorough search, from the kitchenette drawers and cabinets to the shelves in that closet."

"And?"

"No Maxwell cassette tape."

"Damn."

"*But…* I found two little cassette players and some cables that could be used for dubbing. And half a carton of blank Ampex tapes, each one still in its plastic wrapper."

Excitement colored her voice. "Which means copies of the sex tape had probably already been made."

"And the guy who jumped me may have gotten them."

"Could have found the original, too."

"Yes."

"Who sent the guy, Mike? Any idea?"

"Several. But all I have to work on is that he had dark eyes, a decent build, and was maybe as tall as me."

"Sounds like a real brute... Mike, I have another call. That's the number from Pat's car phone! I better take it."

She was gone for almost thirty seconds. I was just starting to think we'd been cut off when she was back.

"That was Pat," she said. "He's at the scene, outside the Flatiron Building—on Broadway. There's been a hit-and-run. Mike... it's the Long girl! Lisa Long's been killed."

I swallowed. "Stay put, kitten. I'm heading there."

A sob caught in her throat, but she got the words out: "Mike, does murder *have* to follow us?"

"No. But we have to follow it."

The shouting, like they say, was over by the time the cab dropped me on Broadway outside the Flatiron. No ambulance, just a squad car pulled over to block a lane of traffic, its cherry top whirling. The sad chalk outline of a sprawl that had been a young woman's body could be seen, as could the dark Rorschach stain of blood that the outline didn't contain. Two uniformed officers were still at the scene, one on the sidewalk and another in the street. A plainclothes man was questioning shell-shocked pedestrians.

One of the uniforms, Manny Romero, recognized me and told

me where I could find Captain Chambers. Romero was middle-aged and said, "I see you still wear a hat. Weather like this makes me think I should dig one of mine out."

The sky was grumbling and night was moving in early.

I said, "They issue a hat and a trenchcoat, you know, when we take out a P.I. ticket."

That amused him, barely. "Is that right?"

"What do you make of this one? Straight hit-and-run?"

"I would've said that," Romero said. "But the newsstand guy? Claims the car accelerated. He hit that poor girl like a torpedo."

"'He'?"

"Some baby-faced teenager. Rebel without a clue. Out gettin' his kicks, little fucker."

I nodded, patted the cop on the shoulder, and headed across Broadway.

When I went through the revolving doors into the narrow lobby, Pat was over at left, notepad in hand, interviewing the fifty-ish uniformed guardian-at-the-gate behind his little white desk. In a raincoat and no hat, the big rangy blond captain of Homicide heard me come in, wrote down a few final notes, nodded in curt thanks to the interviewee and tucked his spiral pad away. Then he walked out of the guard's earshot and summoned me with a curled finger.

When he got a closer look at me, Pat asked, "What happened to you?"

He meant the nasty hematoma at my left temple.

"Like Dino says," I said, "ain't that a kick in the head."

His chuckle was dry. "From this afternoon, huh? You should get that looked at."

"I didn't know you cared."

Pat nodded toward the guard at the desk. "Just picked up an interesting tidbit," he said. His smile was the kind that went well with hard, irritated eyes.

"Must be gratifying when that happens," I said pleasantly. "So little wheat and so much chaff in an officer of the law's day."

He ignored that. "Seems the late Erin Dunn's section of the building to clean included Senator Winters' office. That's Senator Jamie Winters, whose secretary became a hit-and-run fatality a little over an hour ago."

"Now you're going to remind me," I said, "that I asked the Super for Erin Dunn's contact information the other day."

The grin didn't pretend to be anything but sarcastic. "Oh, I thought we might skip that and go right to a phone call I got from a Detective Brice over in Brooklyn."

I folded my arms and gave him a nice friendly smile. "So that saves me from having to fill you in about that little incident."

"That 'little incident' where three people got killed and you had a run-in with their killer? No. I'm up to speed, thanks. We can jump right to where you tell me how this all connects up."

The best way to handle a smart cop is to answer a question with another question. Or two. "Have you talked to the senator? Was he still here when this happened?"

"He was. He still is." Pat nodded upward. "He's waiting in his office because so far I've only interviewed him in the most perfunctory way. You see, he saw it happen."

"Oh?"

Pat nodded. "He'd been chatting with the Long woman outside

the building. End of their workday, see-you-tomorrow kind of thing. She was heading to a bus stop and he was about to go the other direction to a parking garage. He saw her cross the street, in the middle of the block, and she turned to wave, and he waved back, just as a car came up fast. A big Buick Riviera, dark blue with white trim. Hit her so hard, she flew up and rolled off the hood and windshield, and the bastard went right over her. Some of the witnesses lost their lunch. Some damn near lost their minds."

I shook my head. "I spoke to her yesterday. She was a nice kid."

"Skip it. What I want to know is—was this simple hit-and-run, or just…"

"A hit? A murder? Could be, Pat. Anybody get a good look at the driver?"

"A look, yes, several of the sickened spectators. That's what doesn't feel like anything but a real accident—it was young kid, smooth-faced boy maybe in his teens, in a red stocking cap and a Jets sweatshirt. And here's the kicker—somebody got the license plate number."

"Well, great!"

"Not so great. We ran it and the car was reported stolen earlier this afternoon. Which makes this sound like a joyride."

"Maybe it's supposed to sound that way."

He frowned; all the homicides he'd seen, something like this could still tie his guts into knots. "Mike, what the hell is this about? Where does the senator come in? I've got a hunch *he's* your client. That the murdered cleaning gal and her boyfriend are tied in with, what, blackmail? The senator has a rep as a womanizer."

I gave him half a grin and a shoulder pat. "You'll make a good detective someday, Captain Chambers. Tell you what—let's go up and talk to the senator."

"Yeah. Let's."

"But first, me."

"Whaddya mean, first you?"

I gestured to myself. "Well, let's say, hypothetically, that the senator is my client. In such a case, I'd want to get his permission before answering a question from you about a hypothetical extortion attempt. And maybe other information that I couldn't otherwise reveal."

Pat was quietly steaming. He knew about my arrangement with a lawyer in the Hackard Building that gave me attorney/client privilege with all of my clients. Knew damn well it was standard with me.

"All right," he said, sighing. "We'll go up. You can have a few minutes with your… hypothetical client. I'll even let you sit in on the interview… but I'm asking the questions. Understood?"

"Understood. You're the law enforcement professional, after all."

That actually made him laugh. Nice to see his mood improve so quick.

So we went up to the nineteenth floor and Pat stayed out in the hall and had a smoke. He'd quit that nasty habit more times than I had, and was between tries at the moment.

I found my client sitting behind his secretary's desk. He was slumped there, leaning on his elbows, hands covering his face. Hearing me come in, the hands lowered but the elbows stayed put. His green eyes were bloodshot and his perfectly barbered dark brown hair had an atypically unruly look. The dark gray suit coat of a tailored number was still on, but the pink-and-white tie around the white collar of his pale gray shirt was loose, a knot the hangman hadn't snugged yet.

The boyishly handsome face looked its full early-forties reality for a change. "Mike... what are you doing here?"

"I guess you could say I'm reporting in." I sat in the visitor's chair opposite him. Tugged back my hat.

"What happened to you?" he asked, nodding toward the black-and-blue blossom to one side of my forehead.

"Turns out not everybody likes me," I said.

He didn't know what to make of that.

I folded my arms again, put an ankle on a knee. "You got lucky. Captain Chambers is a friend. Probably my best friend in the world. Or we wouldn't be having this pre-interview chat."

"Captain Chambers... he... he *already* interviewed me."

"That was just the warm-up. You're in for more, maybe much more. I don't have to level with Chambers for him to find out what's been going on. He's already jumped to blackmail without any help from me."

"I... I can't even *think* of any of this... not after..." He swallowed hard. "I saw her die, Mike. I saw that car come roaring out of nowhere and then she was just... in the air... and then... you could hear the crunching... bones... things inside her..." He covered his face, shuddering, shivering.

"You should save that stuff for Chambers. I don't have time for melodramatics, whether they're sincere or not."

The bloodshot eyes flared and he leaned back in his dead secretary's chair. "Are you accusing me of...?"

"Nothing. I believe you cared about that girl." I believed he cared about all of those girls, in his way. "But right now, Jamie boy, I need instructions from you, and you need some from me."

"In… structions?"

"How much do you know about what's happened today?"

He said his wife had informed him that the cassette tape that ex-Governor Hughes had sold us was a copy.

"What else is there to know?" he asked hollowly.

I told him that I had spoken to the governor this morning and revealed to him that Erin Dunn and her boyfriend had swindled him. That Hughes had hired me to handle the situation, including preventing his exposure and likely arrest as a blackmailer. When my client started to react, I added that the governor's fee would be contributed by me to the Vankemp Foundation.

Then I told him about my second visit to the brownstone in Park Slope.

"Three dead," he said, his expression glazed.

"And me damn near dead," I pointed out.

He threw his hands in the air. "What the *hell* is going on, Mike?"

"Well, I don't think it's a coincidence that your secretary was a vehicular homicide victim the same day Dunn and Licata were shot to death. And neither does Captain Chambers. Understandably."

He was sitting forward now. "You think the same person killed all three?"

I shrugged. "The same person could be responsible, but a grown man killed that couple, and some young male was behind the wheel when Lisa Long got hit. And in the latter case, 'hit' is the right word. Someone likely contracted both kills. Someone connected. Someone with money."

He winced in thought. "Could the governor be cleaning up after himself?"

"That thought has occurred to me. He doesn't seem the type, but then he's a politician… no offense."

"None taken. So what about those instructions you have for me?"

I held up a "stop" palm. "Don't withhold anything from Chambers. But don't offer him anything, either—make him ask. Let him dig for his share of our taxpayer dollars."

He nodded, his eyes sharp now.

I continued: "Specifically, keep the governor out of this… unless the captain directly asks. You received an anonymous blackmail call. You hired me and I learned that Dunn had stolen the tape. Leave it at that, if you can."

"What are you going to do, Mike?"

"Well, the governor and I are going to talk again. But I have a few other things in mind to do first. For now, I'll sit in on the interview with Chambers. I'll give you an occasional prompt. Okay?"

"Okay."

So Pat came in and I kept my chair while the Homicide captain made a looming presence, trying to intimidate a man who met important people every day, including his own damn wife.

Jamie was properly upset about the accident, but avoided melodramatics, and in a fifteen-minute interview that covered no new ground at all Pat didn't ask about the governor. Apparently he was still in the dark there.

I had bought myself a little time.

CHAPTER ELEVEN

The Caffe Reggio on MacDougal Street in the Village was in business a good twenty years before I was. Some said neither one of us had changed much since. And my porkpie fedora and trenchcoat were pretty much the same, even if personally I was considerably more weathered.

As for the Caffe Reggio, it still boasted the same sagging ceiling, elaborately framed paintings, old clocks on wall pedestals, dim lighting, folk music, and green walls as ever. Like the lines in my face, the cracks in those walls lent what they call character. Same was true of the ceiling fan that could have been a prop out of *Casablanca*, and was, or the espresso machine dating to the turn of the century that cost the original owner of the café a cool grand in 1927, back when that was real money.

Half of a wide, ornately carved wooden booth, with two small round marble-topped tables facing it, was where Velda and I and three young women with whom Senator Jamie Winters had enjoyed carnal relations were currently in conference. We fit in fine with the mix of aging hippies, over-the-hill bohemians, tourists, and grad-school wait staff.

Of the three young women seated across from us—Velda and I each had a little table to ourselves—I had previously met only Nora Kent, the "blonde" singer from Rose's Turn who'd turned out really to have black, pixie-cut hair under her big frizzy wig. Right now she was wigless, in a blue-and-green plaid shirt and jeans (all three girls were in jeans) that went well with the Reggio's earth tones.

Velda introduced me to the other two—Helen Wayne, who wore a loose dark-green sweater, her hair short and brown and permed; and Judy McGuire, in a jeans jacket over a black t-shirt, her hair long and brown and brushing her shoulders.

I had assigned Velda the task of rounding up the three women for this meeting, and had chosen this spot for a meet because the Village was where they lived and worked. By the time I got there—it was early evening now—all three of the senator's former paramours were present, and so was Velda. The young women, seated in a row like that, were peas in a pod, short but not petite, curvy but not voluptuous, cute more than pretty, none wearing anything but the lightest make-up.

Velda had caught up with all of them by phone at their jobs— the singer at Rose's Turn was also a waitress there—and told each it was vital to come see her, because the blackmail matter with the senator had really heated up.

She did not mention that two others like them would be present, too. Or, for that matter, that murders had been committed. Today.

Now they sat, each nursing espresso cups, eyeing each other nervously, sometimes exchanging twitchy little smiles, but not engaging in conversation. I had told Velda not to tell them what they had in common, but to let them figure it out. They had to know they were of a similar type.

The senator's type.

"Let them squirm a little," I'd told Velda.

And squirming they were, when I'd arrived and settled in my chair.

I nodded to them, said hello, ordered myself a coffee with cream and sugar, then thanked the women for accepting our invitation.

"I'm guessing," I said, "you've figured out what you three have in common."

Helen Wayne blushed. Judy McGuire frowned. And Nora Kent smirked. A sort of human female variation on see-no-evil, hear-no-evil, speak-no-evil.

"Ladies," I said quietly, "I don't mean to alarm you, but another member of your society was a hit-and-run victim today. A fatality. Very likely a murder."

All three looked at me now with identical wide-eyed expressions of alarm. It might have been comical, under other circumstances.

I continued: "Lisa Long, who until her demise a few hours ago was Senator Winters' current secretary, now resides in the city morgue. And as you've no doubt surmised, the Long woman was having an affair with the senator. The blackmailer has a recording of them together. Doing *what*, I believe, can be left to your imagination."

The alarm was gone and various shades of shame, irritation, and regret passed across the similarly cute faces as I continued.

"Two of the parties involved in the blackmail scheme," I said, "were murdered today in Brooklyn."

Alarm returned and, as I spoke, evolved into fear. Not one of the women had as yet asked a question or made a remark.

I said, "Erin Dunn was on the nighttime cleaning staff at the Flatiron Building and is the source of the tape recording. Her live-in boyfriend, Anthony Licata, was part of the scheme. Both were shot and killed in Dunn's apartment late this morning."

That froze them.

Then Judy McGuire became the first to speak up. "This hit-and-run... it's not a coincidence, is it?"

"Not very damn likely," I said. "Judging by the eyewitness accounts, the car was aimed at her like a bullet. A big car going very fast. That makes three murders in one day."

"What's going on?" Helen Wayne asked, her voice quavering. Her eyes looked wet.

Nora Kent said, in a flip way that sounded a little forced, "Sounds like a blackmailer whose plans went blooie is cleaning up after himself. Is that how you see it, Mr. Hammer?"

I nodded. "I believe I know who's doing this, or I should say who is paying to have it done. The Brooklyn murders and the vehicular homicide occurred too close together to've been the work of one individual. Besides which, a man around my size was responsible for the Dunn and Licata killings, while the driver of the hit-and-run car was a teenage kid."

Frowning somewhat suspiciously, Judy asked, "How do you know a man your size killed those people in Brooklyn?"

"I saw him," I said. I pushed back my hat and pointed to the purple splotch alongside my skull. "He gave me this."

Now the women were exchanging glances, suddenly realizing

they were, as I'd put it, part of the same society.

Very business-like, Velda said, "We would like each of you to pack a bag with enough clothes and personal items to last you a few days. We'd like you to call in sick to work. We want to keep you under our protection until this business is cleared up."

Again, the young women exchanged glances, thrown by this suggestion, even confused.

Frowning, Nora said, "For how long? Couldn't an investigation of something like this take months?"

"I move faster than the police," I said. "And with a whole lot less red tape. Since I already have an idea who's responsible, this could just mean a single night out of your lives. If you don't cooperate, however, you might not have any nights left. Or days."

Nora again: "I don't see why we're in any danger. None of us is currently involved with Jamie, are we?"

The other two shook their heads.

Nora picked back up: "And—to our knowledge anyway— there's nothing like that tape you mentioned to tie any of us to Jamie in that way." She looked at the other two. "Is there?"

Again, they shook their heads.

Velda said, "You need to consider the possibility that the senator himself, or his wife, or *both* of them are responsible. If that's the case, you're all very much on the firing line."

Nora was frowning. "I thought you were *working* for the senator and his wife."

"I am," I said. "But if my clients are lying to me, and using me as a stalking horse to clean house… let's just say I won't take it kindly."

"Also," Velda said, "remember that a political figure like the senator has many backers who might take it upon themselves to, as Mike puts it, 'clean house' for their candidate. These are powerful people Mike and I have never even met, let alone know!"

"Which could mean a very long investigation," Nora said.

"Look," I said. "Ladies… things may settle down soon, and as I say, I think I know who the responsible party likely is. And I'll deal with that individual tonight. So, like I said, what we're talking about here might mean one night away from your lives. But we… for now, for *right now*… need to get you out of harm's way. Four murders were committed today. So this is no time to be taking chances."

The three women exchanged unhappy looks.

Velda said, "We have a safe house arranged."

Frowning, Helen asked, "What's a safe house?"

I said, "A secure location, to hide witnesses or other people under threat of violence. We work with a security firm that keeps half a dozen such places available at all times. We've already arranged one."

Velda said, "We can't force this on you. But we urge you to cooperate with us."

I said, "Either Ms. Sterling here or I or both of us will be with you at the safe house at all times. Velda is a licensed private investigator and ex-policewoman. She will be armed and ready. I've been a licensed private investigator since before you were born, and I'm an ex-cop myself. So. What say?"

With a little hesitation, and glancing at each other like they were old friends by now, each in turn either nodded or said "yes" out loud.

"Good," I said. "Now, my car is parked nearby. We'll go as a group. I will take each of you to your own apartment, where Velda will go up with you. I'll stay down on the street with the other two. You'll pack a bag quickly. Call work and leave word, and then we'll move on to the next girl's apartment. Within an hour and a half or so, we should have all of you snugly installed at the safe house."

And that's what we did.

It went smoothly. The safe house was a five-room furnished apartment over a pizza parlor on a cross street near the Garment District. I parked illegally and went up alone to check the place out, finding it empty and clean and ready for us, thanks to the security service. Velda and the three women and their overnight bags went through the door by the pizza place and on up the stairs. I watched the lights go on. After perhaps two minutes, a shade raised and Velda was framed in the window giving me a smile and a thumbs up.

I left the black Ford in a parking ramp a block down, then walked back to the pizza parlor, where I ordered a couple of large pies, making one of them a veggie, since a lot of young women were vegetarians these days. I got one with pepperoni and sausage for Velda and me. I paid and told the clerk I'd be back for them.

Upstairs, each girl had a bedroom to herself in the nondescript but pleasant apartment, quarters that compared favorably to a decent motel. No phones. Radios in each room. The bedrooms fed a living room with a sleeper sofa and a TV, where Velda and I would camp out. The kitchen was small but serviceable. With the girls getting settled in, in their respective quarters, I sat on the sofa next to Velda.

"The Security Services boys did good," I said.

Velda nodded. "Even the sheets are clean. Fridge is full, too. Milk's nice and fresh. Even some Miller Lite for you."

She put a hand on my arm, glancing toward the bedroom doors, all of which were shut at the moment, as our tenants made themselves at home. "Mike—did it ever occur to you that you may have let a fox in the henhouse?"

I shrugged. "I think all these little hens are pretty foxy."

Velda elbowed me. "You know what I mean."

"I do know what you mean. What if one of our pretty little gals was in on the extortion scheme? Or even *behind* it? A jealous former lover turned bitter blackmailer? That's why you have to stay alert here at this sorority. You're the house mother, after all."

She was frowning. "What if you really *are* a stalking horse in this thing, Mike? We may have handed two of these three over to a murderer."

Nodding, I said, "Maybe I should search those girls. Yeah, I think a strip search is in order."

She grinned at me and put a fist under my chin. "You think you're pretty cute, don't you?"

I kissed her fist. "No. I just think I know who's behind this thing, and baby, it makes me sick. Sick to my stomach."

Her features grew serious. Damn near grave. "You think our ex-governor is the man behind the curtain, don't you?"

I nodded. "And I hate the thought. He wasn't strictly my political flavor, but I always took him for honest—for a politician anyway. My idea of a rare straight-shooter in that racket."

She sighed and shrugged elaborately. "Hughes had to swim in New York waters, Mike, to get where he got. And you know what kind of waters those are. Full of empty bottles and used condoms and bloated bodies and…"

"You do have a rare line of sweet talk, my love," I said. "But you're right about those waters. Our ex-governor had union backing, going way back, which includes some mobbed-up boys. Our ex-guv could easily have reached out for a hitman or two, untraceable to himself."

"So that's where you're off to, then? To confront the governor?"

"You bet. To the top of the Waldorf. Not their famous Starlight Roof, but an upper floor, all right."

Her dark eyes were zeroed in on me. "But I don't see you trying one of your tricky plays with the likes of him. Harrison Hughes is not going to pull a 'rod' on Mike Hammer and get himself shot in self-defense. And even at *his* age, Hughes is a tough old bird, ex-army colonel that he is. You won't slap him around into a confession, like the good old days."

I nodded. "No, but I can make it clear that the game is up. That all my resources and those of my friends at the NYPD are going to be lined up against him. And that if one hair gets harmed on the pretty heads in those bedrooms nearby, he will be exposed for the monster he is. That he's *become*."

"You seem sure of it."

I shook my head. "No. But I can see it. I *can* see it. In a way, I hope to God he can show me the error of my thinking, and that his explanation isn't wrapped up in a bribe or a threat. That

I *am* wrong about him. That he *is* the good man I always took him to be."

Before I left, I went down and got the pizzas. Soon we were sitting at a table in the little kitchen, one big happy family. The girls were smiling and getting along, and Velda was interacting with them just fine. Like I said, the house mother. And only one of the girls—Helen—was a vegetarian.

Velda dug into the meaty pizza, but I only put away a single slice.

I'd kind of lost my appetite.

A cab dropped me at the Waldorf Astoria, the celebrated and luxurious hotel between 49th and 50th Streets and Park and Lexington Avenues. I'd told Velda where the Ford was parked in the ramp near the safe house and left her the keys, should she need to move our charges or something else unexpected came up.

The Waldorf's mosaic-floored lobby was a mile long, furnished in eighteenth-century English and Early American, and rivaled any cemetery in marble, bronze and stone, and most museums in paintings by famed artists. The hotel's top eighteen stories, of fifty, were twin towers with their own elevator bank. The thirty-fifth floor was where ex-Governor Hughes' residential suite could be found, just down from the Presidential Suite where President Bush and his wife Barbara stayed on Manhattan visits.

The president wasn't on this floor right now, but a uniformed cop was stationed outside the Hughes suite, hands clasped behind him. I didn't figure this was standard security for the ex-governor. Hadn't been this morning.

I approached the uniform, who I didn't recognize—he was a pale young guy with rosy cheeks—and said, "Is there a problem here, officer?"

He raised a palm, like he was working traffic. "This is a crime scene. You'll need to move along, sir."

"What kind of crime scene?"

"I'm not at liberty to say."

I got out the leather fold and showed him the badge and my P.I. ticket. "Son, I'm an officer of the court and Governor Hughes is a client. Who's in charge here?"

The door opened and Pat Chambers filled the space. He didn't even seem surprised to see me. You might even call that thing on his face a smile.

"Thank you, Doherty," he told the young uniformed man. "Mr. Hammer is a friend of mine…. Mike, would you step in here please?"

Within seconds we were sitting on opposing two-seater leather couches facing each other over a low-slung glass coffee table next to the fireplace with its mantel of awards and framed photos of the governor and his family and with a few celebrities. From down at the end of the room, where the double doors onto the dining room stood open, the scurry of technicians and photographers, their flashes strobing, could be heard, but didn't quite tell the story.

But they sure as hell hinted at it.

I said, "Governor Hughes?"

Pat nodded, an ankle resting on a knee, his folded hands on his stomach like Judge Hardy getting ready to give son Andy the facts of life.

With that barely-a-line of a smile riding his lips, he said, "You want to tell me about how the governor fits in with what you've been up to?"

"Is he in the other room?"

"Yeah. I'll give you a look when things settle down. The boys have some work to do."

"Murdered?"

"Apparent suicide."

I thought about that. Shook my head. "No way. Not the kind."

"According to his suicide note, he is."

"Handwritten?"

"Typed."

"Signed?"

He nodded again. "With a scrawl that could be his signature. We'll see what the handwriting expert says about it." The smile grew a little. "Tell me about you and the governor, Mike. You're not quite old enough to retire yet. You might still like to hang onto that license of yours."

I flipped a hand. "Velda has a license. All you need in a little agency like ours is one."

"Tell me, Mike." The same words but with a lot more edge.

So I told him.

Told him how our esteemed ex-governor, against his best instincts and better angels, had stooped to blackmail when he got access to information that could sink the presidential hopes of Senator Jamie Winters. I did not say that the "information" was a tape, but a detective with much lesser skills than those of Captain Patrick Chambers could figure the dead cleaning woman and her live-in boyfriend had got something on the senator in that office she regularly cleaned.

"The senator is your client," he said.

"The governor was my client, too."

"Well, aren't you getting political in your old age. Sounds like a conflict of interest to me."

"It's complicated."

He gave me a scowl the likes of which I'd rarely seen from him. "Do you really think you can hide behind that client confidentiality crap on a *murder* case?"

"I thought it was a suicide."

He talked through his teeth. "Those three dead in Brooklyn didn't kill themselves."

I smiled with mine. "That isn't your case, is it? Don't you work Manhattan?"

He closed his eyes. He left them that way for what seemed like a long time, but was probably fifteen seconds at most. The techs and photogs talking and moving around in the dining room provided background noise. Finally he opened his eyes.

I said, "Aren't those short naps refreshing."

He said, "We believe the Long woman was murdered."

"You're getting good at this, Pat. Live to be a hundred and you'll make inspector. You can skip the 'and-run' and make it just 'hit.'"

"You see hit men in this."

"I did. Not so sure now."

The eyes closed again, but reopened in a few seconds. "Let's hear it."

And I told my long-suffering friend that I had strongly suspected the governor of hiring contract kills on the Brooklyn duo and Lisa Long as well. Such a thing seemed out of character for a man of Harrison Hughes' long public service, and of course he'd been a brave soldier who rose to colonel. But so was blackmail, and he'd gone there, hadn't he?

"So, figuring in his possible mob ties," I said, wrapping up, "with the union backing he got over the years, I figured he was the most likely mastermind here. Cleaning up after himself."

"Now you're not so sure, suicide note or not."

"Now I'm not so sure, yeah."

Pat had a single eyebrow up. "What about your other clients?"

"I'm mulling that."

The captain of Homicide's irritation with me had faded. He got up, gave me a look and a raised finger—not a middle one, either—to tell me to stay put. I obeyed while he walked over and entered the dining room.

A few minutes later the photographers were dispatched by Pat to take shots of the other rooms in the suite, and I heard him send the three techs along as well, to dust the rest of the rooms and their contents for prints.

Then he stepped out from the dining room, curled his finger at me. I got up and followed him into the supposed suicide scene.

The governor, in yellow pajamas and brown slippers, was seated at the dining room table where earlier today he had taken his breakfast. He was slumped over a portable typewriter, head thrust to his right, with a scorched bullet hole in his left temple, flesh stippled with gunpowder. The weapon that killed him had been held close.

That apparent weapon, a nine millimeter Browning, was on the floor with the fingers of the hand at the end of his left arm all but pointing to it. On the wall, on the other side of where he was sitting, was a splash-like bloodstain. On the floor, where they had slid, were chunks of gore in a puddle of grue.

Otherwise the room—the high-end, possibly antique furniture like the china cabinet—were as they'd been this morning.

On the table near his right hand—that arm was flung there—was a typewritten sheet. It said:

"To my friends, colleagues and children—

I have endeavored to be a good man and a responsible public servant. I served my country with distinction. But I have failed of late.

I attempted to bring a good man down. Extortion is a sin that I cannot live with.

Forgive me."

Below was HJH, his initials, in ink—as Pat had reported it, a scrawl—apparently from a ballpoint pen nearby on the table.

I said, "Horseshit."

"I didn't like the smell, either," he said. "What's your take?"

I gave him some of it. "He would never say that he served 'with distinction.' You don't brag in a fucking suicide note."

"Not generally, no. What else?"

What I really didn't like was the repetition of "good man," but I didn't say so.

"Was he left-handed?" I asked Pat.

"No. But a right-hander shooting himself with a gun in his left isn't unknown. Somewhat suspicious is all."

"Okay, but who dresses for bed," I said, "and commits suicide? Maybe somebody taking pills, but nobody else. He was a dignified guy, proud. He would've dressed in a suit and tie like he was going somewhere special. Which he was."

"Go on."

I shrugged. "I never trust typewritten suicide notes. There's a possibility the note had already been typed elsewhere, on the same brand of typewriter."

"That sounds far-fetched, even for you."

I knew what had really happened, but figured to keep it to myself. For now, sending Pat down the wrong path would let me get there first. I'd be helpful but not too helpful....

"The governor lived alone," I said. "Somebody came to the door and he answered it. That somebody either was known to the governor, or just forced his way in. The killer could have held a gun on Hughes and then dictated the note. Made him type it."

Pat thought out loud: "Or the note could have been typed after the kill. Just move the machine away from the corpse, type the thing, put the machine back and the note in place."

"Sure."

Wrong.

But I threw him a bone. "Do you really think a man this formal, this proud, would sign his initials to something so important? Hell no. He'd sign his full signature. To me, that alone makes those initials a forgery even before the expert chimes in."

He was nodding slowly.

"And not address his children by name?" I said. "No, Pat, you were right the first time—it smells."

"Of murder."

"Of murder. Have the neighbors next door been talked to? And across the hall?"

He gestured in that general direction. "The whole floor's been canvassed. Nobody saw or heard anything."

"A nine-millimeter gunshot and nobody *heard* it?"

He shrugged. "These are high-end suites, Mike. Probably close to sound-proofed. I wouldn't make anything out of that."

He wouldn't. I would.

"Seen enough?" he asked.

"More than," I said.

We wandered back into the living room. Pat paused to holler in to the techs that they could have the dining room back any time they chose. He, too, had seen enough.

I was at the door but Pat was right there by me.

"What now, Mike?" he said.

"What do you mean? It's your case."

Now he grinned big. "Right! I forgot. So I don't need to give you the speech about letting me and my people do our jobs."

"Naw. Knock yourself out, Pat."

Those gray-blue eyes bore into me suspiciously. "You walked in here thinking that fine gentleman in there took his own life, drowning in a sea of shame."

"Poetic. But if he drowned in anything, it was his own blood. But me, I'm swimming in that shame sea, my friend. I allowed myself to be snookered into believing our ex-governor was the kind of man who would have others killed to save his own skin, his own reputation. I shouldn't have bought it."

I went out. Nodded to the young cop and headed for the elevator.

No, I shouldn't have bought it.

But somebody was going to buy it tonight.

CHAPTER TWELVE

Streetlights, giving the apartment building's base a jaundiced glow, reached upward to create shadows that made the Dakota seem even more like something out of an old Universal creep show. Skeletal branches from Central Park across the way seemed to extend like the bony fingers of witchy hands casting spells, while occasional lighted windows stared back unblinkingly like random yellow eyes. The tan-and-brown-edged building loomed like a mammoth gingerbread house suggesting yet another witch might wait within.

The cabbie, whose name on the little card by his picture was a mess of consonants in search of a few more vowels, said, "So many famous people live at this place. Why here?"

"It's a museum," I said. "And they're the exhibits."

He nodded. That made sense to him.

I was still on the visitors' list and the uniformed doorman was damn near friendly this time, and didn't even mind when I asked him a few questions. I got the answers I hoped for, and rewarded him with a five-spot. His grin told me the rich-and-famous tenants probably weren't as generous. They almost never were.

I made my way through the tunnel-like entry to the nearest of the four corner elevators. Up on the seventh floor, the gloom of the corridor was offset by the feeling you were walking around inside some fine antique. The place even smelled like yesterday.

I used the buzzer at the door of Judy Garland's former digs. It took a couple of tries before Nicole Winters—having checked the peephole—flung that door open wide. No ponytail today—all that red hair was spilling around her shoulders, so carelessly, perfectly arranged—and the moist red of the lipstick on her wide, full mouth had an orange cast. That went well with her trademark green, this time expressed by a loose-fitting, low-necked lime silk blouse, untucked, and emerald velvet slacks, her feet bare and barely showing, the dark green eyes big and wide, a fashion accessory in and of themselves.

But, at the moment, an alarmed one.

My hat was in my hands and she all but shrieked, *"Mike!* What *happened* to you?"

I gave her half a grin and gestured to the hematoma. "Somebody tried to kick some sense into me. Sorry to just drop by."

"Come in! Come in!" she said, gesturing with a green-nailed hand, holding the door open wide. "Let me take your coat."

I let her hang it up and the hat, too.

"Jamie told me about that poor woman at the office," she said, frowning sadly, shaking her head, red hair dancing on her shoulders. "Imagine getting run down by some hopped-up kid! It's getting to where you can't cross a city street and not be at risk."

"Pretty brutal out there, yeah."

The closet-lined hallway, all that dark wood a ghost of the

original apartment, gave her elbow room enough to walk at my side and slip her arm through mine, escorting me along with a lovely smile. She didn't seem to be mad at me anymore for turning down the offer of her body.

"If you came to talk to Jamie," she said, "I'm afraid you're out of luck. He's off at some political affair."

Always one affair or another for Senator Winters, I thought.

She was saying, "A testimonial dinner for a state congressman or something. As a rule I skip that kind of thing. Just not devoted enough a wife, I guess."

"It's you I wanted to talk to, anyway."

She smiled, pleased. "Oh. All right. Shall I fix us drinks?"

"Sure."

She did that at the wet bar while I plopped down on the pop-art sofa in the vast white living room, which was illuminated by subtle track lighting, neither bright nor dim. I unbuttoned my suit coat, getting comfy… including easy access to the .45 under my left arm. The curtains were pulled back to reveal the windows on Central Park by night, street lamps throughout all the lush greenery glowing like stationary fireflies while well-lit roadways made veins of winking light coursing through the darkness.

The sky over the park, hovering above the city like a threat, was a dark charcoal mass of moving clouds, with thunder distant but ever present. Little bursts of electricity crackled and sparked and disappeared, adding gold filigree momentarily to what might have been dirty industrial smoke.

Somehow Nicole summoned music on an unseen sound system—Miles Davis, "Lift to the Scaffold"—and then delivered me a CC and ginger, bringing along a glass of white wine for herself. She sat near me—on the red center cushion—and propped those bare feet of hers on the table. Even her damn toenails were green—lime, like her blouse. She was wearing no bra under it and her nipples dared me to notice, the curves of her breasts peek-a-booing at the edges of the low, tear-drop neckline.

She seemed to be over the death of that "poor woman."

I asked her, "When did you last speak to your husband?"

She shrugged. "On the phone. He was at the office. A police captain named... Chandler was it?"

"Chambers."

"This Captain Chambers wanted to talk to Jamie."

"So the senator didn't mention to you what happened in Brooklyn."

She sipped wine. Looked at me, only mildly interested. "Why? Nothing ever happens in Brooklyn. Did something happen there anyway?"

So I told her, and she quickly got more than mildly interested. I told her about the dead landlady, the murdered blackmail couple, and how I'd been jumped by their balaclava-sporting killer. Miles Davis accompanied me with a particularly mournful trumpet.

"Which is how I got *this*," I said, pointing to my purple badge of courage.

"Well, my husband and I had *nothing* to do with any of that," Nicole said, as if discussing a poorly decorated room.

"I didn't say you did."

"You certainly can't suspect me, or Jamie, or the *two* of us of anything as... as *despicable* as that."

171

I smirked. "That word despicable always makes me think of Daffy Duck. Lisp it for me, why don't you?"

She ignored that and shook a finger at my chest and her forehead frowned. "Who you should *talk* to is that self-righteous hypocrite Harrison Hughes! *Think* about it, Mike. You exposed his blackmail and you unmasked his accomplices. He's covering up! And murdering to do it. You know, he has the connections to have it done! They say he was always in the mob's pocket."

Miles had gotten very jazzy now, really up-tempo.

"Do they?" I said. "Well, just the same, I can't go after him."

"Because he's a big shot?"

"No. Because he's dead."

The green eyes goggled at me and her orange-red mouth dropped open like a trapdoor. *"What?"*

I repeated it.

"…How? *When?* My God, Mike—what the hell is going *on?*"

She was trying really hard, and Miles had gotten mournful again; still, it just wasn't playing.

But I went along. I said, "I'd say somebody—or some-*bodies*— are panicking."

She tried confusion. "Where did you hear about this? It wasn't on the news!"

"I saw it." I nodded vaguely in the direction of the Waldorf. "I just came from the scene of the governor's supposed suicide."

Somehow the eyes got even wider. "He *killed* himself?… What do you mean, 'supposed'?"

"It was a fairly clumsy job."

I sipped my drink. I'd watched her mix it, by the way. Unless she pre-doctored the Canadian Club and/or the Canada Dry, I hadn't been slipped a mickey.

I went on: "I figure you dictated the note. Didn't sound like Hughes—bragging before he blew his brains out? Not his style. But calling your husband a 'good man,' with the governor admitting he himself had failed to be one? That sounded like something you'd come up with. Also, the guv would've had a word or two for his kids. Addressed them by name, not just 'my children.'"

She was sitting on the edge of her couch cushion, torso swung toward me, her chin high, her eyes slitted now as they gazed down at me. "This is nonsense, Mr. Hammer. Ridiculous, libelous nonsense."

"Not libel. It's not in writing." I shrugged. "Slander maybe. Conjecture surely."

The beautiful face was frozen now. "I suggest you stop this insulting performance right now."

But I didn't. And Miles picked the tempo back up, urging me along.

"Now, I could call that Captain Chambers you mentioned... he's a buddy of mine, I was just with him, over at the late governor's suite... and I could suggest he get a warrant to shake this little pad of yours down. I have a feeling he might find a typewriter of the same brand and model as the portable Hughes supposedly used. It's probably in your live-in help's room right now. Even with identical models, the forensics guys will be able to tell which machine that note was typed on. How you knew what brand the governor used, I don't know. Wouldn't have been a hard piece of information to come up with."

The lovely features thawed just enough to allow in the slightest smug smile. "You want to call your police captain friend? I can show you to the phone, if you like. Go on. Let him get his warrant."

My smile went full-tilt grin. "Ah. So you've disposed of the typewriter. Well, I shouldn't be surprised. You're anything but a fool. You probably disposed of the silencer, too."

"Silencer?"

I pawed the air. "Oh, please, honey. The governor has neighbors all around him, but *none* of 'em heard the blast of that nine mil? Don't insult my intelligence, such as it is."

An orange-red smile taunted me. "Just who was my accomplice in all this flawed cleverness? My husband, I suppose?"

"In the planning, yes. In the execution? Your majordomo, of course. Andrew Morrow shot Hughes—in the left side of his head, which was also a goof, but never mind—and then dropped the gun there by the dead man's limp fingers. If it's the same weapon that killed the Brooklyn pair—in which case ballistics will easily show it—that might tie the governor in. Might not hold up, though. Hughes is, or was, a public figure and could easily have been seen. And he would've had to make it to Brooklyn before I did."

Miles had settled down again.

"Unless," she said, her expression amused, her air somewhat regal, "he sent one of his mob friends. And, Mike—I can provide an alibi for Andrew."

I nodded. "And he for you, right? That might play. Where is he, by the way?"

"It's his night off."

"Good to know. Means we can get cozy here in your little studio apartment with its romantic park view, if some dark sky doesn't dampen things. Maybe we could light one of the fireplaces. You can strip down again and see how you do this time. Honey, we're going to be great friends."

I leaned over and surprised the hell out of her by giving her a great big kiss. When I withdrew, it made a Dinah Shore smack and everything, and left that perfect orange-red mouth a little smeared.

"Are you insane?" she asked, quietly, as if she really wondered.

"That's been an issue over the years," I admitted. "Look. You're my client. I'm on your side. Frankly, with the kind of money you have, I'd be on your side even without those killer looks of yours. So you spent some of that loot getting rid of some low-life blackmailers? Do I look like I give a damn?"

Miles and me were just grooving along now.

Her eyes narrowed, half suspicious, half hopeful. She was studying me the way a cancer doctor does a critical slide.

"As for the governor," I said and shrugged, "he paid his money and he made his choice. He tossed away everything he ever said he believed in, and threw in with a couple of penny-ante blackmailers. Don't look for me to squeeze a tear out for that slob."

The truth? I already had. And Harrison Hughes was no slob.

She was almost squinting now, trying desperately to bring me into focus. "What are you saying, Mike?"

I put a hand on her thigh. Squeezed. Stroked. "I'm saying I'm on your side, doll, as long as we can come to terms. Now, I'm no blackmailer myself, but I am here to help. Or I will be if you can clear up one thing."

"What would that be?"

I frowned, just a little. "That Long girl. Lisa Long. Why did she have to die? Wasn't the poor woman, as you put it, just another victim in this blackmail set-up?"

She shook her head. "That was an accident. A hit-and-run. A terrible coincidence."

"You expect me to believe that?"

"It's the truth." Her chin came up again. "I swear I had nothing to do with that. And there's one thing I have to make clear. My husband wasn't part of this."

"Really?"

Her nod was firm. "Really. I acted in what I thought were his best interests. Perhaps… perhaps foolishly." She drew a deep breath, then let it out; she was trembling. "But I only meant to clear out this blot on him and his reputation. To sweep this blackmail… and these blackmailers… away."

"Nothing to do with wanting to be First Lady someday."

That chin came up again. "My husband has a great future ahead of him and *of course* I want to be part of it. But that's only part of why I'd do *anything* it takes for him to *have* that future."

Now I was doing the studying.

I'd encountered a lot of people willing to do a lot of things in my many years dealing with the darkness in human beings. But this was a whole new kind of crazy.

Finally I said, "All right. Let's say I buy all that. That still leaves us with four murders. *Somebody* has to go down for all this. And I elect your precious Andrew Morrow."

Her head moved slightly to her right. Softly, she asked, "Why Andrew?"

"Baby, come on. You need to level with me. I can *already* identify him. Where do you think I got *this*." I pointed to the purple patch on my skull again. "He killed those two amateur-night blackmail artists in Brooklyn, and before he left, he found the original tape and a bunch of dupes. Selling him out should be no problem for you, unless he tucked one of those copies away as an insurance policy."

Blue notes from Miles now.

She shook her head. Her voice was almost a whisper, as if she were keeping a secret, when she said, "No. No, he's loyal. He... well, Andrew loves me. And as far as he's concerned, I love him. He knows that Jamie and I, we... we have an arrangement where certain of our needs are concerned. In the larger sense, we're partners in..."

"Crime?"

"Politics. We both believe strongly in the social causes we support. Whatever our... personal peccadilloes might be... our intentions are... pure."

Not only could she say that with a straight face, she really seemed to believe it.

I said, "I never heard murder called a peccadillo before. But okay. As for the Morrow kid, he could come in very handy for our purposes."

"How is that?"

I opened a hand. "Well, he's the actual murderer, isn't he? The Dunn woman and her bartender beau are both on his score card—not to mention the occasional crushed landlady skull—and he did in the governor, not all that long ago. Witnesses probably saw him at the Waldorf. I can I.D. him in Brooklyn. He was in a stocking mask, but I can say I recognized him from his eyes and build.

What's a little white lie here and there? All *you* have to do is tell the truth, more or less. That he was obsessively in love with you, and when the governor and that Brooklyn pair tried to blackmail you, he flew into action on his own volition... totally unprompted by you and your husband, of course."

"But the blackmail..."

"What precisely Hughes intended to blackmail you over will be lost in the shuffle. And the police will cooperate. They'll have no appetite to take on a U.S. senator! It'll be a snap to make that go away."

"You really think so?"

I nodded. "The original cassette tape is gone and, if you're right about your loyal lapdog, all the dupes are, too. You could be in the clear. It's an old term, but it's apropos—you and Jamie need a fall guy. And Andrew would do just fine."

"You can't expect Andrew to go along with that," she said, bending close, voice low. "Not even if I arrange a lawyer who could get him off on an insanity plea or some other technicality, or sneak him out of the country, when he's out on bail. And he *knows* things! If he talked... no. No, this will never work."

I gestured to myself. "Again, do I look like somebody who trips over the niceties of the law? Do you know how many bad guys in my storied career I've put down and called it self-defense? And that pretty-boy son of a bitch kicked me in the head, remember! We rig something up, I put Morrow out of his misery, and presto, a gun suddenly appears in his cold dead fingers. You could even witness it!"

That was his cue.

I figured he'd hear it and respond. I knew he was in the

apartment—the doorman had seen him leave and come back, with the timing right for Morrow to get to the Waldorf and stage the suicide, and then get back afterward, before I dropped by.

And when I'd been invited in, Nicole had practically shouted my name, and she had been far more loudly concerned about my bruised head than she had any reason to be… *not unless she was warning her little lover boy to run off to his hidey hole.*

But I figured the house stud would be eavesdropping, and I was right, because here he was.

Staggering out in a gray designer suit, light gray shirt, and dark gray tie that he'd almost certainly worn to blend in when he went to the Waldorf earlier. But Andrew Morrow clutched something in his hand he would not have carried openly through the hotel lobby…

…a gun.

A Browning 9mm again. Obviously his weapon of choice. The handsome, chin-dimpled mug under the slicked-back black hair wore the kind of devastated, disappointed look kids have when they learn Santa is a hoax.

He moved toward us in a slow lurch, almost dancing to Miles in a slow-motion free-form number.

"Nicole… you *couldn't* do what he says." Morrow swallowed. Shook his head. "You couldn't *do* that to me."

She had turned around on the couch when she heard him enter, and was on her knees on the lower cushion, as if begging or maybe praying, leaning her elbows against the upper one, hands clasped. "No! No, of course not, darling! I was just… just…"

"Stringing me along," I said, turning to look at him casually as he approached where we sat, coming up from behind us. "Maybe

179

she was. Or maybe she was going to rat you out. Anything you say about all this would sound like the ravings of some obsessive lovesick loon."

"Shut up!"

"Or maybe she'd just serve you up to me for slaughter."

"Shut up!"

He came at me faster than I figured, and was swinging the gun-in-hand to smack me with it, when he should have just fired at me—not that it would have done any good because I leapt over the back of the couch and flung myself at him, taking him down, and sending the couch over with me and onto its back, spilling Nicole, sending her tumbling and crying out, to land in a pile on the floor. I was on top of the bastard then, jamming a forearm into his throat, producing a choking gurgle, while with my left hand I had his wrist, the wrist that went with the fist that had the Browning in it. He was strong, and younger than me, and it was my left against his right, which gave him the advantage as we waved it around. He was forcing the snout of that gun toward me, with some success, but when it went off, the bullet flew between us, right past me like a rocket taking off, the explosion of it turning my ears to a whining near-deafness, but I heard her gasp just the same, when the bullet hit.

I didn't *see* it hit, but I saw *where* it hit, in her throat as she sat awkwardly on that bone-color floor, the entry wound like a shimmering ruby in a necklace at the hollow of her neck, and I saw too the blood stream out of the back of her, scarlet with particles of bone from a shattered section of spine. She fell back, like a hinge had broken, and her hair surrounded her like a crown of flames until it quickly soaked in her blood and became just one damn grotesque mess framing a face that somehow still managed to be lovely, though the green eyes had filmed over and couldn't even see the ceiling they were staring at.

Both of us, the majordomo and I, froze, taking this in, but he recovered faster, shoving me off and scrambling across the floor toward her. As I got to my feet, he scooped her in his arms, saying, "*Darling!* No! *Not you!* No!"

Then he lay her down quickly but gently and there was nothing handsome about the teeth-bared face with the wild dark tear-oozing eyes in it when he rose and began to raise the Browning and aim it at me, unsteadily, but aiming it nonetheless.

"You've killed her! She's dead." Like Nicole had been the Wicked Witch of the West and not the toast of the East Side. "I'm going to make you *suffer....*"

Enough of this shit.

I yanked out the .45 and drilled the idiot in the head.

CHAPTER THIRTEEN

Leaving the scorched odor behind, I found a phone on the wall of a kitchen that was as white and modern as the living room. The entire apartment seemed at odds with the Dakota's *Addams Family* motif, although the fresh corpses did fit in.

I called the Waldorf's switchboard and asked to be put through to the governor's suite, figuring Pat would still be working the crime scene—I was right, because Pat himself answered.

"This is Captain Chambers with the NYPD. Who is calling?"

"Pat," I said, "I hate to tear you away, but I have two more dead bodies you might find interesting. One is Nicole Winters, whose Dakota Building penthouse this is—residence 72. The other is her male secretary, who killed those people in Brooklyn and staged the governor's suicide."

"Mike!"

"I can just call the Homicide Bureau or you can take it yourself. Dealer's choice, buddy."

Even on the phone you could tell he was talking through clenched teeth: "What the hell have you done *this* time... 'buddy'?"

"Be easier to walk you through. Phone won't do it justice."

I hung up. Grinned. Nice to be able to do that under these circumstances.

But I had barely hung up, my hand still on the receiver, when the damn thing rang again and made me jump.

I started, "Look, Pat—"

But the familiar voice that interrupted was not the Homicide captain's.

"Who *is* this?" Jamie Winters demanded.

"Oh. Senator, this is Mike Hammer." I made a quick decision to keep him in the dark... and away from the Dakota. "There's a situation here. The police are headed over, Captain Chambers specifically. Looking into a certain blackmail matter and a suspicious suicide."

"What the hell is going on? What are you *doing* there?"

"Advising you as a valued client, I would strongly suggest that you stay away from home base right now. I can explain my presence and everything else, but first I have to deal with Chambers and the cops and talk my way out."

"I want to speak to my wife."

"She can't come to the phone right now." Well, she couldn't. "Look. We need to meet tonight. Let's say midnight. Somewhere private and out of the way."

A tortured sigh. "Well... my unfinished office at the new Vankemp Building should do. It worked *before* as a secure location."

"And it'll work again," I said. "See you there. If I'm late, hang around. Give me at least an hour. I don't know what I'm in for at this end with the cops."

I hung up. I just stared at the phone for a long ten seconds, in case it was in the mood to ring again and scare the crap out of me. It wasn't. It didn't.

But my mind was racing. I had things to do. I had those young women to protect. If I stayed around here and talked to Pat, it could take hours. I might even get hauled over to One Police Plaza and checked into a private room, and it wouldn't be a penthouse. Couldn't be having that.

On the counter near the wall phone was a yellow pad of Post-it notes with a pen. I huffed a laugh and grinned again as I wrote: "Had to run, Pat. See you tomorrow. Love, Mike." I tore the note off and went out into the living room. Strolled over and pressed the Post-it note to the chest of the late Andrew Morrow, who was staring up at the ceiling like the other corpse lounging out here.

After getting into my hat and trenchcoat, I slipped into the hall, snugging the collars up. The doorway down the way opened and a petite attractive Japanese woman, who I'd never met but immediately recognized, peeked out. I got a glimpse of a black-and-red silk kimono.

"I hear something," she said.

"There's been a shooting," I told her. I got out my leather fold and held the badge up for her to see, and from where she stood it must have seemed legit enough. "More police are on the way, ma'am. Everything's under control."

She nodded and sealed herself back up.

I didn't blame her for being gun-shy.

A cab wasn't hard to catch and within half an hour I was sitting on the couch with Velda in the outer area of the safe house, our backs to the tight-shut doors of the rooms of our female guests, the lights out here dim, the TV aglow with Johnny Carson going but the sound way down.

I was in my shirt sleeves, tie loose, and she was in gray sweats—clothes she could sleep in but didn't have to change if something sudden came up. Nothing had so far.

It took a good half hour to fill her in on the events at the Dakota. She stared at me through the telling, rarely blinking, but never interrupting.

Her arms were folded, her gym-stockinged feet on a divan, her dark eyes wide as she looked at me. When I was done, she said, "You're going to be in a lot of trouble, Mike, leaving the scene of a crime like that."

"Don't sweat the small stuff, baby. Bigger fish to fry and all that." I was seated the same way, arms folded, feet up, shoes off. "Something Nicole Winters said is bothering me."

She smirked. "No kidding. *Everything* she said is bothering me."

I shook my head. "No, what I mean is… she started out lying, then essentially copped to being responsible for the Brooklyn murders and faking the governor's Dutch act. She claimed to the end that it was all her doing, with her boy toy's help. Insisted that her husband had nothing to do with the killings. Had nothing to do with trying to erase everybody and everything, on and surrounding that sex tape."

Now she was shaking her head. "But why would Nicole stop lying only to tell the truth about everything except *that*? Why would she go to such lengths to protect her husband?"

I shrugged. "Because she loved him. Jamie screwed around on her, yes, but with her blessing, and she herself seemed to consider sex just another flavor of aerobic exercise. But the bottom line, baby, is she loved the guy."

Velda smirked again, this time accompanied by her eyebrows going up. "Well... women *have* been known to fall in love with cheating bastards before."

I half-smirked. "Let's not get personal, doll."

"Didn't mean to cross the line."

I shifted my position to look right at her. Really lock eyes. "But there's *something* in all those lies and truths Nicole spun for me that really sticks out."

"You'll have to point me to it, Mike, because it's all one big blur in my brain by now."

"The only murder Nicole didn't openly cop to was Lisa Long's. She even seemed... emphasis on 'seemed'... to think it might really have been an accident."

Velda squinted at me. "What do you make of that?"

I shrugged a shoulder. "Not sure. It doesn't jibe with her insistence that the senator wasn't part of the killings that she and the majordomo hatched. Because if she really didn't know that the Long hit-and-run was a murder, that indicates her husband arranged it. *Without* her knowledge."

Velda nodded again. "Because otherwise she'd have taken the blame for *that*, too."

"Right."

"So what does it all mean, Mike?"

"I'm not sure. But one thing jumps out about that kill—the 'hit man' was a kid. A fresh-faced boy. What kind of hired killer is *that?*"

She couldn't tell me.

I got up, stretched, and went for my coat and hat. I was almost out the door when Velda was right there, handing me something.

She smiled just a little. "You don't want to forget this."

"No," I said, tucking it away in my suit coat pocket. "I don't. I'd sooner leave my .45 behind. Which I'm not about to."

I told Velda to keep an eye on our slumber party participants while I made one last call on this very long day and night.

At the Vankemp Building construction site.

The rain finally came.

Had it been any colder, it would have been snow or sleet or even hail again. Thunder roared like King Kong and lightning curled its ragged spooky fingers while the wind seemed to be angry that just about everybody had made it inside, leaving the streets and sidewalks as close to empty as New York ever gets.

The downpour was brief, the onslaught starting in just as I was climbing into a cab outside the safe house. By the time I reached the stretch of Fifth Avenue where tenements used to rule and which now was home to high-rise wealth, the attack was over, with only the wind remaining to let you know who was boss. It whipped at my trenchcoat and made me hold my hat on as I approached the chain-wire fence. A few last bursts of electricity were reflecting off the sixty-story glass-and-steel obelisk of the Vankemp Building like a lighting effect in a dance club.

Nothing had changed but the newly added pools of rainwater around the construction site grounds, the machinery huddling under skins of raindrop-pearled plastic, tarps shielding them in anticipation of the sky exploding, a promise that had been kept. The Caterpillar tractors looked like oversize pooches that had forgotten how to shake the wetness off after an unwanted bath.

The chatty old cop at the chain-link fence's gate recognized me and let me in without fanfare. Still dripping from the cloudburst, he was not in the mood to talk tonight. Some cardboard sheets spread around outside the multiple entry doors allowed me to wipe my feet after the walk across the muddy work area. The old boy unlocked the glass door and let me in, managed a damp smile and a nod, then disappeared.

The smell of rain had found its way in to mingle with the glue and paint odors of a building in progress. The somewhat dirty, tile-floored lobby looked the same as a few days ago.

A few days ago! Was that really all it had been? So much deception, so much corruption, so much murder! And in so short a time?

Full circle so soon, pushing the up button, stepping on the elevator, using the key I'd held onto to access the sixtieth floor. Whisked up to an unfinished lobby with bulging plastic over uninstalled windows and those autopsy-like hanging veins and arteries of wiring dangling over uncarpeted floor. Knocking at a mahogany door that said SENATOR JAMIE B. WINTERS. And without saying a word, hearing, "Come in, Mike!"

Was I here again, or just still here?

Again, Jamie Winters was behind the makeshift desk of plywood and sawhorses, seated on a stool, with a metal stool waiting opposite. He wore a very conventional but clearly tailored charcoal suit, padded shoulders the only fashion concession, with a white shirt, collar open, no tie in sight. His boyish countenance could have stood a shave—it had been a long day for him, too—and his dark hair's hundred-dollar cut had been mussed some by wind before he got here.

Right now the dazzling white smile had been put away. His expression was business-like with a dollop of skepticism, and maybe a hint of anger, his forehead and eyebrows tight. No bottles of Canadian Club and Canada Dry awaited me this time. No wrapped hotel-room glasses. He had a cigarette going in the ashtray, a pack of Salems nearby.

He gestured to the stool. "Sit. Please."

Another stool had been pushed to one side. I slipped out of my trenchcoat and draped it over the seat, set the porkpie fedora on top. It was cold enough to leave them on, but I thought I might not want to be encumbered. I unbuttoned my suit coat. I sat.

The floor-to-ceiling windows at either side of the room were fluttering, or anyway the plastic was where soon glass would be, sometimes expanding, sometimes contracting, like this large, mostly empty office was a living, breathing animal. A dangerous one.

"I heard on the radio," he said.

"What did you hear, Senator?"

"That Governor Hughes is dead. Unconfirmed sources are reported as saying it's suicide. Was it *you*, Mike?"

That surprised me. I admit it. I gestured to myself as I said, "Me? Hell no."

One eyebrow went up. "You must admit it *sounds* like you. And if you've overstepped your role in so ghastly a fashion, as my representative? I am having *none* of it."

I almost laughed. That was good. He was smart. Turning it around on me like that? With that touch of righteous indignation? There was a natural politician sitting across from me, all right.

"I had nothing to do with that," I said. I held up a palm, as if swearing in at court. "Let's make some ground rules. I'm here to report on what I know. May take a while. When I'm done, ask whatever questions you like."

He thought about that, or anyway pretended to. Then he nodded and said, "Fair enough."

"Before we get into that, I have sad news. Senator, I'm sorry to have to tell you… but your wife has been killed."

There was no pretending in his reaction. He was genuinely astonished. Quickly, eyes flaring, he said, "Who did it?"

I hadn't said she'd been murdered. I might have meant it was an automobile accident—like the one Lisa Long died in, only not a contrived one. Or maybe she slipped in the tub and cracked her skull—a bathroom is the most dangerous room in the house, you know.

But he went right to murder.

"In a way it was accidental," I said. "Her accomplice, Andrew Morrow, came at me with a gun. We struggled, and he fired the thing and a stray bullet took Nicole down. I'm sorry. It was quick. You need a minute?"

Senator Winters took a few seconds, then shook his head. His jaw muscles were flexing; it took the boyishness away. He reached for the cigarette and sucked on it, let smoke out, then returned the cig to the tray.

He said, "I am going to ask a question, Hammer—fuck your ground rules."

"Okay."

"What do you mean, Morrow was her 'accomplice'?"

"Earlier this evening, Nicole confessed to me that she was attempting to protect you by getting rid of Erin Dunn and Anthony Licata. An innocent bystander, their landlady, was also killed by Morrow. What you heard about on the radio, our ex-governor's 'suicide'? That was Morrow's work, too. The police are well aware he faked that. They will soon know, if they don't already, that Nicole was involved."

Winters had started shaking his head halfway through that. "Foolish damn woman. Goddamn her." He swallowed, held back tears, or gave that impression. "God love her…"

"Question is, did *you* love her?"

Choking back what might have been a sob, he said, "Very much. I'm sure the… unconventional nature of our relationship is something… something you can't grasp. But yes, I loved her."

"Well, she loved you, all right. She really did. Oh, she loved the idea of being a '90s version of Jackie Kennedy, too. But she truly believed in you. Believed in the social issues and concerns you espouse."

He was nodding somberly. "I'm sure she did."

"And I believe—I really believe—that if the terrible things she undertook for your benefit would've been exposed, she would have fallen on her sword for you. Right up to its emerald-studded hilt."

His head went back and his eyelids went up. "What do you mean, 'my benefit'?"

"As much as the role of First Lady was something she hoped to inhabit, and even to redefine, she wanted most for you to be president. Even if she couldn't be at your side. She'd take the blame. The fall. For everything you did."

"What did *I* do?"

I gestured to him. "Only everything. *You're* the chess master. She was your queen, all right, but ultimately the queen is just another game piece on the board."

His eyes were narrow now and he spoke through a slit of a mouth. "What exactly happened tonight? At the penthouse. *Do you still work for me or not?*"

"Sure I do."

"Then tell me. In as much detail as you like. I won't interrupt. Your ground rules, Hammer."

So I told him. Writing up my cases as I have over the years has developed in me a fairly remarkable recall, and I was able to repeat what both of us said, more or less. Just as I've given it to you.

"I fail to see," Jamie Winters said, after another drag on that cigarette, "how anything Nicole said incriminates me. She did, as you say, take the blame for all of these foolish actions."

"Actually," I said, "it's one 'foolish action' she *denied* doing that most incriminates you."

"Is that right?"

"It is. She denied having anything to do with the Lisa Long hit-and-run kill. She even seemed to think it might really have been an accident."

"And how is that damning to me?"

I shrugged. "Why should Nicole deny that one murder? She took responsibility for all the others. That would seem to indicate *you* hired the 'accident' done."

That rated a sneer. "'Seems' is hardly proof."

"You were right there at the scene, Jamie, outside the Flatiron. Chatting with the woman on the sidewalk. Were your eyes on that car, parked down along the curb? Its driver waiting for the traffic to thin enough for you to signal it to pull out? Or were you just waiting for that speeding car to come into sight and then distract Lisa and send her on her way… to her death."

Winters shook his head and shrugged at the same time. "Not proof. What do you want from me, Hammer? What are you after?"

I beamed at him. "Money would be a start. This began with blackmail. Let's end it that way. With Nicole gone, you're going to be a very rich man. You could keep me on retainer. Say $100,000 a year? I could be your damage control guy. I have a feeling you have a lot of damage that could use controlling."

The senator studied me. Studied me for a very long time— probably thirty seconds, which is an eternity. Try it and see. Time it on your watch.

Then, slowly nodding, he said, "All right. All right, Hammer. I think you may just be the man I could use, long-term. Could I hire you through that attorney you work for? To keep the client confidentiality intact?"

"You bet. But tell me something."

"Certainly."

"Why keep Nicole in the dark about Lisa Long?"

He shrugged. "It came up rather spontaneously. When the blackmail scheme seemed on the verge of exposure, removing Lisa from the scene… in an accident… made sense. I don't relish having that done. I was fond of the girl. But in a larger sense, she was expendable."

I waved a hand, like a diner at 21 summoning the check. "I thought you were a romantic, Jamie. That you loved these women… as long as the affairs lasted, anyway."

His smile was a mildly self-mocking thing. "I *am* a romantic, actually. I do love them, usually. Lisa… well, she was convenient. How can a man resist a beautiful secretary like that, particularly one as interested in you as you are in her?"

"Tell me about it," I said with a smirk. "One thing. What about the *other* girls? The ones you and Nicole gave me to check into? I hope I haven't been… well, the phrase 'stalking horse' has come up. I wouldn't like to see wholesale slaughter become the policy where all your former girlfriends are concerned."

He raised a "perish the thought" hand. "Certainly not! Am I some kind of monster? No, Lisa had to go because she'd become intertwined with this blackmail business—a victim, like myself, but caught up. The other girls whose names Nicole gave you, well, that was before we knew whether any of them might be involved in this blackmail scheme. No, they're quite safe."

"What if any of them came forward at some future date?"

He batted that away. "I don't believe any of those three would dream of embarrassing me or themselves. I can't imagine it from them." He shrugged. "Of course, if any of them should… misbehave… accidents *do* happen. And I'd have Mike Hammer on staff to deal with it, wouldn't I?"

We exchanged smug smiles. Two men who wouldn't murder a woman unless they really had to.

"Since you've made a confession of sorts," I said, with an embarrassed shrug, "perhaps I should do the same."

He was stubbing out his cigarette in the tray. "Oh?"

I reached in my right-hand suit coat pocket and withdrew the object Velda had passed me on my way out of the safe house: the same little metal-case cassette recorder that, at the Dakota the other day, I'd used to play the sex tape for Nicole's entertainment and edification. Or I should say, a dupe of the sex tape.

I said, "For the record… and this recording… I hereby state I have no intention of taking a yearly retainer from Senator Winters, and my offer to do his dirty work was simply a method of getting him to own up to what he's done."

"Goddamnit!" he blurted, halfway off the stool.

The .45 came out from under my left arm so fast even I was impressed. With my free hand, I stopped the cassette recorder and popped the little gizmo with the tape still in it in my suit coat pocket.

"Thank you, Senator," I said.

The wind outside was such that I hadn't heard the elevator ding and the doors slide open. Of course, I hadn't been listening for it. But *somebody* had been listening for a while—at the door to the senator's office.

Somebody named Nora Kent.

"Put down the gun, Mr. Hammer!"

Very carefully, slowly, I craned to look back at her.

She was in jeans and an untucked pink-and-white plaid flannel shirt open over a gray t-shirt, both hanging over her jeans. She wore no make-up and her black hair was so short, she might have been a boy. Had she tucked it under a stocking cap, and with no make-up, she'd have looked even more like a boy.

A teenage boy.

The kind who might go out joyriding in a stolen car.

She had a gun in her hand. It wasn't as big as my gun, just a Baby Glock, but it could shoot nine-mil slugs and if we've learned anything here, it's that a nine-mil slug can kill you very damn dead.

She was twirling the forefinger of her left hand as she gave me orders: *"Hold the butt by two fingers! Put it down! Don't throw it!"*

She was smart. She knew that if I dropped the .45, particularly dropped it hard, the thing might go off. So I knelt. And put it down, gently, by two fingers. Then stood again, slowly.

"Jamie," she said, in her breathy Julie London voice, "what should I do with him?"

Winters was holding his hands up, palms out, almost like he was the one being threatened by a woman with a gun.

"Don't kill him here," he said. "We'll take him down and get him out and away somehow. We'll have to get past the security guard."

She shook her head. "I already took care of the geezer."

Winters frowned. "How hard did you hit him?"

"I didn't hit him, I shot him. The wind covered it. He's dead." She shrugged. "He had a nice long life."

Winters frowned, but any regret was a momentary thing.

I was facing her now. "So what's this about, honey? Getting a recording contract through Jamie's show biz contacts? Or maybe *you* want to be First Lady, too?"

Her teeth were small white feral things. I hadn't noticed that before. And her eyes—those oh-so-blue eyes… Christ, they were crazier than mine!

"I want it all, Mike!" she said, her smile shining with greed. "But there's something I want that you would never understand…"

"What's that, baby?"

She grunted a laugh as her little automatic stared at me with its black noncommittal eye. "'Baby,' 'honey,' 'doll'… what a cornball old creep you are. Do you even *know* what love is? Or is it all just rutting to you? What do I *want*? I want Jamie Winters, you fool. Because I *love* him, and he loves me. Have you even *heard* of that?"

I had, but I also heard something she hadn't, because this time I'd been listening for it. The elevator. I'd told Velda not to fall asleep till I got back. I'd told her that if one of the girls ducked out, she had to follow that girl. Because one of those dolls might have been eavesdropping when I filled Velda in and mentioned the meeting with Winters at the Vankemp Building. Because I may be dumb, but I'm smart enough to know a young woman with no make-up and a stocking cap pulled down can pass for a teenage boy, particularly in a car speeding by. And I figured one of those cute hens in our charge really might be a fox….

Winters came around the makeshift desk. He stood next to me, at my left, taking me by the arm. Said to her, "Go get that big gun of his and hand it to me. He's a tricky mother. Both of us need to cover him when we go down."

Nora nodded and was keeping her Baby Glock trained on me as she came over to my right to lower herself and reach for the .45, where I'd dropped it a few feet away.

"Put the gun down, Nora!"

Velda, a goddess in gray sweats, was standing just inside the unfinished office, that little hammerless .32 of hers in one sweet hand, its barrel pointing like a scolding finger at the petite crouching singer, who had not yet retrieved the .45.

"*Do it*, Nora! A gentle toss!"

Nora, her cute face ugly with hate, pitched her Baby Glock off to one side, nice and easy.

"Good girl," Velda said, holding her position.

That was when Nora went for the .45, coming up with it in her two hands, springing to her feet and charging at Velda, firing wildly. The thunder of it rivaled anything the sky had produced on this terrible night, but the rounds only chewed up the senator's mahogany door, because Velda had already hit the deck.

And when my raven-haired partner's .32 barked a bullet up into the songbird's chest, spinning her around to face Winters, my gun fumbling from her uncaring fingers, Nora Kent looked at Jamie Winters in desperate love and sudden pain, reaching her arms out to brace herself or perhaps embrace him.

Horrified, the senator tried to back away only to bump into the bulging plastic covering a window where glass wasn't yet, popping it like a blister, and they both tumbled through, letting screaming banshee wind in, her limp form chasing him as he windmilled face-up, all the way down, the bloody stain on her back a ragged valentine, his scream not dying until he did.

Then Velda was there hugging my arm, looking at the tiny torn figures in the construction rubble below, the plastic they'd taken with them providing no cushion at all, just flapping around them in the wind that whipped Velda's hair and my suit coat, as well.

"Don't say it," Velda said.

"What, that they really fell for each other?" I grinned at her. "Wouldn't dream of it."

TIP OF THE FEDORA

Although the intent here has not been to create an historical mystery novel, my approach does attempt to place each of these collaborations in the context of when Mickey Spillane wrote the material I worked from, and where in Mike Hammer's life the tale occurs.

(By the way, do not be tempted to do the math about how old Mike Hammer, Velda and Pat Chambers are in the novels set from the 1980s through the early twenty-first century. Mike Hammer ages, but not in the same way as the rest of us. He has more wiggle room than we do.)

To provide a background at least somewhat consistent with reality, I leaned upon research, most of it on the Internet. The major articles I used for this purpose in *Murder, My Love* are: "How Brooklyn Got Its Groove Back" by Kay S. Hymowitz, *City Journal*, Autumn 2011; "Singing a Sad Song for Their Piano Bar" by Anthony Ramirez, *New York Times*, July 19 2007; "The Old Duplex" in *Vanishing New York* (Dey Street Books, 2017) by Jeremiah Moss; "Roberta Flack Price Chops Co-Op at the Legendary Dakota Building in New York City," *Variety*, January

19, 2017; "Visiting Caffe Reggio" by Jen Carlson, December 8, 2014, *Gothamist* website; and "Secrets of the Flatiron Building" by Michelle Young, November 24, 1918, *New York News*. Additionally, I referred to the book *"21: the Life and Times of New York's Favorite Club* (1975) by Marilyn Kaytor.

My thanks to publisher Nick Landau and his editorial staff at Titan Books, including Ella Chappell and Davi Lancett, for continuing to pursue what has been termed the Mickey Spillane Legacy Project. The wide and warm response to the Spillane Centenary publications in 2018 and '19 has been gratifying to those of us who consider the writer (he abhorred the term "author") one of the major figures of tough crime and mystery fiction.

Toward that end, Jane Spillane—Mrs. Mickey Spillane—has made all of this possible. And Mrs. Max Allan Collins—writer Barbara Collins—has served as my in-house editor, cheerleader, and critic, making several plot suggestions along the way.

Finally, my longtime friend and agent Dominick Abel continues to be indispensable where his clients Mickey and Max are concerned.

ABOUT THE AUTHORS

MICKEY SPILLANE and **MAX ALLAN COLLINS** collaborated on numerous projects, including twelve anthologies, three films, and the *Mike Danger* comic book series.

SPILLANE was the bestselling American mystery writer of the twentieth century. He introduced Mike Hammer in *I, the Jury* (1947), which sold in the millions, as did the six tough mysteries that soon followed. His controversial P.I. has been the subject of a radio show, comic strip, and several television series, starring Darren McGavin in the 1950s and Stacy Keach in the '80s and '90s. Numerous gritty movies have been made from Spillane novels, notably director Robert Aldrich's seminal film noir, *Kiss Me Deadly* (1955), and *The Girl Hunters* (1963), in which the writer played his own famous hero.

COLLINS has earned an unprecedented twenty-three Private Eye Writers of America "Shamus" nominations, winning for the novels *True Detective* (1983) and *Stolen Away* (1993) in his Nathan Heller series, and in 2013 for "So Long, Chief," a Mike Hammer short story begun by Spillane and completed by Collins. His graphic novel *Road to Perdition* is the basis of the Academy Award-winning Tom Hanks/Sam Mendes film. As a filmmaker in the Midwest, he has had half a dozen feature screenplays produced, including *The Last Lullaby* (2008), based on his innovative Quarry novels, also the basis of *Quarry*, a Cinemax TV series. As "Barbara Allan," he and his wife Barbara write the "Trash 'n' Treasures" mystery series (recently *Antiques Wanted*).

The Grand Master "Edgar" Award, the highest honor bestowed by the Mystery Writers of America, was presented to Spillane in 1995 and Collins in 2017. Both Spillane (who died in 2006) and Collins also received the Private Eye Writers life achievement award, the Eye.

MIKE HAMMER NOVELS

In response to reader request, I have assembled this chronology to indicate where the Hammer novels I've completed from Mickey Spillane's unfinished manuscripts and other materials fit into the canon. An asterisk indicates the collaborative works (thus far). J. Kingston Pierce of the fine website *The Rap Sheet* pointed out an inconsistency in this list (as it appeared with *Murder Never Knocks*) that I've corrected.

M.A.C.

*Killing Town**
I, the Jury
*Lady, Go Die!**
The Twisted Thing (published 1966, written 1949)
My Gun Is Quick
Vengeance Is Mine!
One Lonely Night
The Big Kill
Kiss Me, Deadly

*Kill Me, Darling**
The Girl Hunters
The Snake
*The Will to Kill**
*The Big Bang**
*Complex 90**
*Murder Never Knocks**
The Body Lovers
Survival... Zero!
*Kiss Her Goodbye**

MIKE HAMMER

The Killing Man

Murder, My Love*

Black Alley

King of the Weeds*

The Goliath Bone*

MURDER NEVER KNOCKS

MICKEY SPILLANE & MAX ALLAN COLLINS

A failed attempt on his life by a contract killer gets Mike Hammer riled up. But it also lands him an unlikely job: security detail for a Hollywood producer having a party to honor his beautiful fiancée, a rising Broadway star. But it's no walk in the park, as Hammer finds violence following him and his beautiful P.I. partner Velda into the swankiest of crime scenes.

In the meantime, Hammer is trying to figure out who put the hitman on him. Is there a connection with the death of a newsstand operator who took a bullet meant for him? A shadowy figure looking for the kill of his life?

"This novel supplies the goods: hard-boiled ambience, cynicism, witty banter, and plenty of tough-guy action."
Booklist Review

"Max Allan Collins was an ideal choice to continue the bloody doings of Hammer."
The Washington Times

KILL ME, DARLING

MICKEY SPILLANE & MAX ALLAN COLLINS

Mike Hammer's secretary and partner Velda has walked out on him, and Mike is just surfacing from a four-month bender. But then an old cop turns up murdered, an old cop who once worked with Velda on the N.Y.P.D. Vice Squad. What's more, Mike's pal Captain Pat Chambers has discovered that Velda is in Florida, the moll of gangster and drug runner Nolly Quinn.

Hammer hits the road and drives to Miami, where he enlists the help of a horse-faced newspaperman and a local police detective. But can they find Velda in time? And what is the connection between the murdered vice cop in Manhattan, and Mike's ex turning gun moll in Florida?

"[O]ne of his best, liberally dosed with the razor-edged prose and violence that marked the originals." *Publishers Weekly*

"For Mike Hammer's fans—yes, there are still plenty of them out there—it's a sure bet." *Booklist*

"It's vintage peak-era Spillane so seamless it's hard to see where the Spillane ends and the Collins picks up." *Crime Time*

For more fantastic fiction, author events, competitions,
limited editions and more

VISIT OUR WEBSITE
titanbooks.com

LIKE US ON FACEBOOK
facebook.com/titanbooks

FOLLOW US ON TWITTER
@TitanBooks

EMAIL US
readerfeedback@titanemail.com

VISIT THE AUTHOR'S WEBSITE
maxallancollins.com